CALL[...] KILLER

"The Wrath is coming," Slade added. "Yessir, the omnipotent Wrath."

Slade let loose with a fiery tirade about the mark of the Beast, making no sense that Fargo could discern. Then he finally gave his "preaching" a pulpit pause.

"Jack," Fargo said, "what's going to happen next Wednesday?"

"What won't happen? Yessir, screwed, glued, and tattooed. The whole city."

"Now you don't sound like a preacher—just a murderer."

"Too late to reform me. I've already killed twenty-seven men."

Fargo wasn't eager for a draw-shoot with this inveterate killer. But he was nearly convinced by now that Slade wasn't bluffing about next Wednesday. Sometimes a man had to choose the lesser evil.

Fargo twirled his six-gun back into its holster. "Care to try making it twenty-eight men, Jack?"

THE
TRAILSMAN

#354

NEVADA
NIGHT RIDERS

by

Jon Sharpe

A SIGNET BOOK

SIGNET
Published by New American Library, a division of
Penguin Group (USA) Inc., 375 Hudson Street,
New York, New York 10014, USA
Penguin Group (Canada), 90 Eglinton Avenue East, Suite 700, Toronto,
Ontario M4P 2Y3, Canada (a division of Pearson Penguin Canada Inc.)
Penguin Books Ltd., 80 Strand, London WC2R 0RL, England
Penguin Ireland, 25 St. Stephen's Green, Dublin 2,
Ireland (a division of Penguin Books Ltd.)
Penguin Group (Australia), 250 Camberwell Road, Camberwell, Victoria 3124,
Australia (a division of Pearson Australia Group Pty. Ltd.)
Penguin Books India Pvt. Ltd., 11 Community Centre, Panchsheel Park,
New Delhi - 110 017, India
Penguin Group (NZ), 67 Apollo Drive, Rosedale, North Shore 0632,
New Zealand (a division of Pearson New Zealand Ltd.)
Penguin Books (South Africa) (Pty.) Ltd., 24 Sturdee Avenue,
Rosebank, Johannesburg 2196, South Africa

Penguin Books Ltd., Registered Offices:
80 Strand, London WC2R 0RL, England

First published by Signet, an imprint of New American Library,
a division of Penguin Group (USA) Inc.

First Printing, April 2011
10 9 8 7 6 5 4 3 2 1

The first chapter of this book previously appeared in *Bitterroot Bullets*, the three hundred fifty-third volume in this series.

Copyright © Penguin Group (USA) Inc., 2011
All rights reserved

Ⓟ REGISTERED TRADEMARK—MARCA REGISTRADA

Printed in the United States of America

The Trailsman

Beginnings ... they bend the tree and they mark the man. Skye Fargo was born when he was eighteen. Terror was his midwife, vengeance his first cry. Killing spawned Skye Fargo, ruthless, cold-blooded murder. Out of the acrid smoke of gunpowder still hanging in the air, he rose, cried out a promise never forgotten.

The Trailsman they began to call him all across the West: searcher, scout, hunter, the man who could see where others only looked, his skills for hire but not his soul, the man who lived each day to the fullest, yet trailed each tomorrow. Skye Fargo, the Trailsman, the seeker who could take the wildness of a land and the wanting of a woman and make them his own.

*Comstock Lode, Virginia City, Nevada Territory, 1860—
where warpath Indians, gold lust, and a doomsday prophet
pile on the agony for Skye Fargo.*

1

Skye Fargo hauled back on the reins, staring at the grisly abomination tied to the wheel of an abandoned freight wagon.

"Steady, old warhorse," he said, calming his nervous stallion as it stutter-stepped away from the sickly-sweet smell of death. Fargo removed his hat to whack at the flies thickening the air.

Lips forming a grim slit through his cropped beard, the man some called the Trailsman studied the corpse bound to the wheel. The man had been shot so many times that Fargo couldn't count the bullet holes. But the shots had been carefully aimed so that death would not be quick. Both ears had been sliced off—a violent signature that Fargo recognized.

"Looks like Terrible Jack Slade's handiwork," he remarked to his black-and-white Ovaro. "This could get interesting."

It was Fargo's policy to bury any dead man he chanced upon so long as the deceased hadn't tried to kill him. But the mess on the wheel made his stomach churn. He booted his horse forward, eyes closed to slits against a merciless sun blazing in a hot blue sky. Virginia City, mountainside home of the gold-and-silver-rich Comstock Lode, lay straight ahead—a mining-town hellhole he would normally avoid like a cholera plague if a good friend hadn't asked for his help.

The majestic Sierra Nevada range of California rose high to the west, throwing its only spur into Nevada Territory. Fargo had been riding the federal road from Fort Churchill since sunup, pushing his luck. Three nomadic tribes—the Bannocks, the Shoshones and the Paiutes—had been on the scrap against white men since the Pyramid Lake Uprising, just last year, that slaughtered more than eighty white skins.

A half hour later Fargo rounded the shoulder of Mount Davidson and saw Virginia City spread out before him. It looked surprisingly like a real town complete with false fronts and plank-board walkways. The Comstock lay at the foot of the town in Washoe Valley. Fargo had just reached the outskirts of town when an astonishing sight made him rein in: about a dozen women came running along Center Street, naked as newborns.

Fargo was pleased but not baffled: the infamous "running of the whores" was a daily ritual in Virginia City to advertise the carnal wares and get the miners all het up. He nudged the Ovaro aside to let them pass.

"Hey, Buckskins!" called out a buxom redhead as the girls flew past. "It's on the house for you and those dreamy blue eyes. Ask for Trudy at the Gold Room."

"A stallion riding a stallion!" chimed in a petite blonde with a corn silk bush. "Ask for Jenny at the Wicked Sisters saloon. I'll climb all over you."

Fargo doffed his hat. He knew that most men—himself definitely included—needed to cut the buck now and then. But these gold grubbers on the Comstock didn't just raise hell—they *tilted* it a few feet.

Fargo heard bells clanging from the Washoe, the steam skips that took men deep down into the stopes, or mine chambers, where gold and silver were extracted from the veins. Trees were scarce and signs all over town warned WATCH YOUR LUMBER!!! Evidently the signs weren't much use because Fargo could see that boards were missing everywhere.

He spotted a small cubbyhole office with the words VIRGINIA CITY JAIL painted on the door. Fargo reined left, swung a long leg over the cantle, and landed light as a cat. He wrapped the reins around a hitch-rack fronting the building and pulled his brass-framed Henry rifle from its saddle scabbard. Then he went inside.

The moment he entered Fargo saw a sturdy, earnest-looking young man seated at a battered kneehole desk sorting through a stack of wanted dodgers. He had a strong jaw and a part in his hair straight as a pike.

"Marshal Jimmy Helzer?" Fargo asked.

"Right down to the ground," the lawman confirmed, his tone friendly but guarded. "Friend or foe? From the look of you, I hope it's friend."

Fargo laughed. "Any kid brother of Captain Pete Helzer is definitely my friend."

Jimmy's eyes brightened and he stood up, offering his hand. "Ah, hell, I should have known you, Mr. Fargo. Wearing buckskins, carrying a brass-frame Henry, that Arkansas toothpick in your boot. And I'll bet you rode in on a first-rate Ovaro. Pete told me you were riding dispatches between Sacramento and Fort Churchill."

"That's the way of it," Fargo confirmed.

Jimmy's eyes clouded with suspicion. "Say, did Pete send you up here because he thinks I can't handle this job?"

Fargo chuckled. "Son, does your mother know you're out? *No* one man can handle this job. I read in a San Francisco newspaper that the Comstock produced more wealth in the past year than the entire nation. All that color ups the ante on violence. You need at least five deputies. Hell, last time I was here Virginia City was just an empty mountainside with one steep mule path."

"Things change fast in a boom. Now we have thirteen thousand people, forty stores, twenty-five saloons, and one hundred well-built homes."

Jimmy pointed Fargo to a chair and perched on one corner of the desk. "We've got more than a few pick-and-shovel millionaires running around town. But for every man who strikes a bonanza, twenty more go bust and get desperate. And the ones who do strike a lode are lucky to hang on to their claims."

"These new corporation fellows, right?"

"Yep. Last year, one of those slickers from New York got a man named Jay Kajewski tanked and bought his claim for five thousand dollars. It has since produced two million dollars in gold. Men who won't sell meet with 'accidents.' "

None of this was news to Fargo. Out on the frontier nothing was cheaper than a human life. Killing didn't carry the stigma it did back east. Most murders weren't even investigated or ended in acquittals. A man was far more likely to hang for horse theft than for murder.

"Yours is no job for a featherbed soldier," Fargo agreed.

"I'm a fair-to-middling hand with firearms," Jimmy added. "But this town is cram full of gun-handy murderers and shake-

3

down artists hungry for easy money. And these prospectors and miners are a strange, half-civilized bunch. We've had two shooting affrays already today and it's barely past noon. When I tried to find witnesses everybody suddenly went blind."

"Boomers," Fargo said, "are the same everywhere—profit quick and move on. All they've ever known of 'law' is badge-happy bullies, so they don't trust it. And it can't help that you have Terrible Jack Slade to wrangle."

Jimmy looked uneasy. "You know him?"

"He doesn't exactly stand in thick with me, but I know him and I'm glad we've never locked horns. He could make Satan himself step off the sidewalk."

"I won't lie to you, Mr. Fargo. The man fair gives me the fidgets. He's crazy as a shitepoke as soon as he gets a couple under his belt—and as dangerous as a sore-tailed bear."

"Turns into a kill-crazy marauder," Fargo agreed. "I take it you know about the . . . thing tied to a wagon wheel south of town?"

Jimmy nodded, worry suddenly molding his young face. "Slade's work, all right. I just don't know how to handle him."

"Neither do I, so I just let him be. When he's sober he's friendly and mannerly—hell, even gentle. But firewater transforms him. Far as I know, though, he never bothers decent people."

"No. And even though I suspect him of six killings since he got here, every damn one *needed* killing. Rafe Jennings, the body you saw, was wanted for raping and killing a thirteen-year-old Chinese girl."

"Glad I didn't bury him," Fargo said.

Jimmy chewed on his lower lip. "Pete told me this job is too much for me. Wants me to go back to farming in Iowa. I'm from a village called May Bee. Only criminal I know of back there was a barn burner."

"You're free, white, and twenty-one—that's your decision, not Pete's. But he told me you were once a sheriff in Placerville."

"Constable, actually."

"If it pounds nails, it's a hammer. By any name, a man has to use his fists and his wits to keep a Sierra mining camp in line. And the Comstock is worse."

4

"Well . . ."

"Jimmy, law can't be perfect in a hellhole like this. If you push too hard, you'll be murdered. Say, do you like a stiff belt now and then?"

Jimmy looked embarrassed. "Whiskey gives me dyspepsia. I like a cold beer though."

Fargo pushed to his feet. "I need to cut the trail dust. What's the best saloon in town?"

"Well, the Wicked Sisters is the cleanest. It's on the south side of Center Street—long wooden awning out front."

"Tell you what," Fargo said. "I have to put up my horse, so why don't you meet me in twenty minutes or so at the saloon? I'll stand you to a drink and we'll palaver a little more about this Sodom."

"Sure," Jimmy said, "I could use—"

Outside, a crackling volley of gunfire erupted. Jimmy didn't look the least bit surprised.

"Celebration fire," he remarked. "Some lucky bastard just hit pay dirt. He'll be even luckier if he can hang on to it."

Fargo trotted his stallion down wide and dusty Center Street, amazed at how Virginia City had mushroomed since he had last been here two years earlier. He was astounded to see a small public library, although the building stood empty. At the east end of town he spotted a combination smithy and livery barn.

As he tugged rein and crossed the hoof-packed yard, he heard the piercing ring of a hammer on an anvil. Fargo lit down and led the Ovaro inside, spotting a heavyset man with hairy hands shaping a horseshoe on the anvil.

"What can I do you for?" he greeted Fargo, studying the Ovaro's impressive muscle formation. "Finest-looking horse I've seen in a long time."

"He'll do to take along," Fargo agreed. "As soon as you can, would you give him a feed and a rubdown? And can you board him for a few days?"

"Be a pleasure. Prices are steep, though. Dollar a day."

Fargo nodded. That price was indeed steep, but he expected it in a thriving gold town. He stripped the saddle loose and threw it over a saddle rack, hanging his bridle over the horn.

After a quick washup at the pump in the yard, Fargo headed

down the plank walkway toward the Wicked Sisters saloon. Along the way drunk, wild-eyed miners and prospectors, some armed like Wells Fargo guards, staggered out of saloons, eyes seeking trouble. But one look at Fargo's granite-chiseled, sun-bronzed face and fearless gaze made them veer away from him.

Fargo slapped open the slatted batwings of the Wicked Sisters and entered a crowded, smoke-hazed, raucous barroom. A hurdy-gurdy machine sent out its mechanical version of music, produced by the friction of a rosined wheel on the strings. Fargo noticed that some of the men, clothes stained red with ore, wore knuckle-dusters—loops of heavy, shaped brass wrapped around their hands. Drinking jewelry, soldiers called them, and Fargo knew a solid blow could kill or cripple a man.

He spotted Jimmy at the long counter of raw milled boards. The kid wasn't too green, Fargo realized—he was standing with his back to a wall and he could see anyone who came in.

"Brother," Fargo greeted him, "you've chosen a hard way to make thirty dollars a month and found."

"Oh, it's a mite more than that. I get a buck and a half for every drunk I manage to buffalo and jug."

A barkeep wearing sleeve garters and a Mormon wreath beard had to lean close so he could hear them.

"Skye Fargo, meet Tim Bowman," Jimmy said. "Best bar dog on the Comstock."

"*The* Skye Fargo?" Bowman asked. "The jasper the newspapers claim cleaned out that gang in South Pass?"

"A newspaperman," Fargo opined, "is a little old lady of both sexes."

Bowman looked apologetic. "I'm required by my employers to notify all new customers: no folding money. Gold and pure silver are all that spend here." He leaned in even closer. "But I'll also accept good nails—there's a serious shortage."

Fargo planked a gold cartwheel. "A shot of whiskey for me and a barley pop for the boy marshal here."

"It's lousy wagon-yard whiskey," Bowman warned. "The red sons have choked off the only supply routes, so we distill our own."

Privately, Fargo suspected the free-ranging tribes in this area had much larger, bloodier ambitions than harassing freighters.

"It's a pisser," Jimmy complained. "We're being slowly choked off. Three months ago you could get any luxury you wanted in this town, even tins of caviar and oysters. And Fort Churchill is only about four hours' ride southeast of here."

"They can't help anybody right now," Fargo said. "Between desertion, disease, and combat casualties almost half of Pete's troop is hors de combat."

Jimmy nodded. "Some of those deserters you mentioned are here in Virginia City, looking for color. I just got a telegram from Pete. The entire fort has only thirty-five effectives, and they can't patrol—they're needed for force protection from hostiles."

"Yeah, and Camp Floyd and Fort Bridger are too far east in the Nevada Territory. Troops would have to cross the Black Rock Desert. The Paiutes and Shoshones are strong now and they'd cut the troops down."

Fargo tossed back the rotgut and tears immediately filmed his eyes as a fiery pit replaced his stomach. "Every word you said is gospel, Jimmy, but before you can organize the louts and hard tails in *this* town to fend off Indians, you'll have to somehow gain control of the worst elements among the residents."

As if in response to Fargo's remark, the entire saloon abruptly fell silent, even the hurdy-gurdy. Fargo watched a dime-a-dance girl's face turn chalk white as she stared at someone outside. The doors meowed inward and a tall, powerfully built man dressed all in black broadcloth strolled in.

"He's on a tear," Jimmy groaned. "Looks mad as a March hare."

Fargo took in the handsome man's silver concho belt, the tied-down Remingtons with walnut grips—and the disgusting necklace of dried, blackened human ears.

"You ignorant bogtrotters!" Terrible Jack Slade said in a voice strong enough to fill a canyon. "Don't you see the Grim Reaper standing before you now?"

The saloon had gone as silent as a graveyard at midnight. Fargo couldn't spot one man with the courage to meet Slade's intense black eyes. Casually, the Trailsman thumbed the riding thong from the hammer of his Colt. But he knew exactly who—and what—Slade was, and Fargo couldn't help an icy nervousness along his spine.

Slade chuckled, his face contorted from the controlled insanity within him. "All right, sheeple, *don't* believe the harbinger of doom. One week from today, anh? Midnight next Wednesday— a beast will rise from the bowels of the earth. And if you are still here, you will *all* be eaten alive!"

2

Terrible Jack Slade's announcement caused plenty of puzzle-headed expressions.

"Has that cockchafer got religion?" muttered a man near Fargo to his friend.

The other man snorted. "Religion? Ah, he's just shellacked and trying to sound like a doomsday preacher. He likes to peddle that line."

Fargo, however, wasn't so dismissive. Clearly most of the men here, while scared spitless by Jack, treated his words as insane babbling. But Fargo knew enough about Slade to feel a deep foreboding. It was a premonition of the lower nerves, not the brain—a cool feather tickling his skin.

"Look sharp, Marshal," he muttered to Jimmy. "He's carrying a heavier load than he can handle, and that means unstable dynamite."

Slade tossed back his head and howled like a wolf. "And the Lord said to them, 'Arise and go to the street called Straight.' Midnight next Wednesday, anh? You've been warned."

"So what's the riddle, Jack?" Jimmy called out in a friendly tone. "We've been warned about what?"

"Helzer, a cowl don't make the monk, and a tin star don't make the man," Jack barked from a face twisted with insolence. "Jack Slade don't crawfish to *no* son of a bitch."

"Everybody knows that, Jack," Fargo spoke up, pouring oil on the waters. "Only a fool would try to humble you."

Slade's mad eyes shifted from Jimmy to the new speaker. When he recognized Fargo some of the insolence bled from his face.

"Well, Skye Fargo. The Prince of Pistoleros, the crap sheets call you. At least there's *one* by-God man in this bunch of bucket bellies. How you making?"

"Right as rain, Jack, thanks. You're looking fit as a rutting buck yourself. Come have a jolt."

Slade's lips spread in a sly smile. "I'll pass, thanks. Duty calls on the man with a mission."

The infamous frontier killer headed toward the batwings, but stopped on the threshold to turn and deliver a parting injunction to the entire saloon: "Hell, we all gotta die once, eh?"

"See?" Jimmy asked Fargo after Slade's melodramatic exit. "See what I'm up against, Mr. Fargo? Claim jumpers and stealers, three tribes on the warpath, and a crazy man who makes my skin crawl."

"Once you mate with despair," Fargo chided him, "you'll be useless. Just hold a steady gait."

Jimmy sent out a long, fluming sigh that blew foam from his warm beer. "I believe that, but . . . do you know what happened when Virginia City recently tried to open a school?"

"Hell, who doesn't? The kids shot their teachers."

"The *kids*, Mr. Fargo. Territorial law barely applies to minors and women. I had to let the murdering demons go."

"Look, you have to pick cotton before you can make cloth. Instead of trying to tackle everything, you take your best odds. Think of it as picking the low-hanging fruit first."

"That's sensible," Jimmy agreed. "But I'm not sure what the lowest-hanging fruit is."

"Snap out of it—it's your job to be sure. Listen, Pete tells me you're an honest man with plenty of courage. But you're only one man against a town full of toughs and hotheads."

"So what do I do? Sit and play a harp?"

"Either quit or stay and do what you can. Pete tells me you try to police everything, even the penny ante stuff. You need deputies for that, so when it comes to the drunk and disorderly and brawlers, I recommend a diplomatic blindness."

Fargo paused to watch a rough-looking man at a table near the sawdust-covered dance floor. He wore sturdy whipcord trousers and two six-shooters tied low in cutaway holsters. Fargo watched him repeatedly finger-snap the wheel of his right spur. Their eyes met and the man averted his gaze.

"Anyhow," Fargo resumed, "you might even have to let some killings go for now. Indians have killed the only circuit judge in Nevada Territory, and boomtown miners' juries almost always go for quick acquittals anyway so they can get back to their claims."

"All that shines," Jimmy agreed.

Fargo laid a dime on the bar and peeled a boiled egg from a bowl nearby. "All right, what's your assessment of the current Indian threat?"

"They've never raided into town—yet. Too many repeating guns here and these tribes haven't got hold of firearms yet. But Bannocks, Shoshones, and Paiutes control the surrounding territory, especially Paiutes. We've had two express riders killed and had to cancel our short-line stage to Sacramento."

Fargo nodded. "All right, that's a threat for sure. But a simple militia can hold the line outside of town until more soldiers are posted."

"That's what I'm counting on. But then there's the little problem of Jack Slade."

"That's a sticker," Fargo agreed.

"You just heard the crazy son of a buck. Sometimes he's a mad dog on a rampage. Wednesday at midnight we'll all be eaten alive. Sure, he says plenty of wild stuff like that. But he's also a ruthless killer."

Fargo's eyes again cut to the hard case in the whipcord trousers. Three men had joined him, and like him neither of them had the look of men who labored honestly.

"Just like the featherheads," Fargo agreed, "Slade is trouble—pure poison. And he always will be until someone kills him. If I was you, I'd start poking into this midnight Wednesday business. But remember that usually Slade only pops over men lower than snake shit."

"I can't gainsay that. He's almost like having a deputy."

"Mm. So from what you've told me, your first order of the day is to concentrate on protecting the smaller prospectors from the big bugs looking to steal their claims."

Jimmy spread his hands in frustration. "Sure, but have you ever gone up against these big mining companies? Talk about throwing sand into the wind. They've got triple the number of thugs on their payrolls than Pete has effectives."

"Speaking of thugs," Fargo said, "that hombre twirling his spur wheel looks mighty consequential. Who is he?"

"Yeah, I saw you watching him. He *is* consequential. His

11

name is Nash Booth. Supposedly he works security for Ephraim Cole, owner of the Schofield mine. But I suspect he's also a night rider for a crooked-as-cat-shit land speculator named Septimus Dunwiddie."

"The Schofield . . . after the Yellow Jacket that's the most productive mine on the Comstock, isn't it?"

"I'll tell the world. Right now it's producing about twenty thousand dollars a day in pure profit."

Fargo whistled. "Is Cole bent?"

"There I'm not sure. But he's also a lawyer, so if he is crooked he knows how to cover it. As for Booth—he likes to work side ventures on his own, and he's tougher than a two-bit steak. Watch him close every minute you're in town. Those three galoots with him—"

"Are his 'private deputies,'" Fargo cut in sarcastically.

"Yeah. Willard Jones, Sam Watson, and Chilly Davis. All four men at that table were court-martialed for stealing U.S. weapons and ammo and selling them to hostile tribes in the Department of Dakota. Oddly, no jail time was involved. Pete says they know names of other soldiers involved in this Indian ring—high-ranking officers."

Fargo nodded. "I place Booth now. He rode with John Brown and his sons and had a hand in stirring up the Kansas troubles back in the summer of fifty-six. I rode into Lawrence, Kansas, only one day after the massacre there."

Fargo fell silent, tasting bile in his throat at the painful memory. The images of decapitated children and disemboweled women were painted on the backs of his eyelids. "Before that," he added, "Booth led one of the scalper armies that sprang up down in Mexico after the war."

"Pete told me about those days. They made two hundred pesos for every Apache scalp they hauled to Chihuahua."

"Apache, huh? Booth *and* the Governor of Chihuahua knew damn good and well that Apache hair was coarse and black just like most of the Mexican peasants—Booth helped clear the land of a revolutionary threat to the Spanish viceroys. Apaches were never the issue."

"Straight goods?" Jimmy demanded, looking startled.

Fargo snorted. "This lad's still got green on his antlers."

"A while ago," Jimmy said, his manner halting, "you mentioned deputies—"

He was cut off when a prospector with a filthy and stained beard, his clothing nearly in tatters, burst through the batwings and loosed a piercing war cry.

"Every swinging dick and every twirling *chiquita* drinks on Bo Gramlich! I've struck a *lode*!"

The saloon erupted in cheers as the opportunistic saloon girls ringed the grinning sourdough. Because of the wretched diet of prospectors, made worse by recent supply woes, Gramlich's raw sunburned face was pocked with scurvy sores. His hands were obviously crippled from hard work.

Fargo watched Nash Booth study the new arrival from lidded eyes. As Jimmy had remarked earlier, Gramlich would be damn lucky to spend the fruits of his labor—assuming that was all he lost.

"Like I was saying," Jimmy remarked awkwardly, "I know that a bunch quitter like you won't pin on a badge, and anyhow, the town charter doesn't authorize pay for any deputies. But maybe you could hire on as a . . . contract roundsman?"

Fargo shook his head. "Pete sent me here to offer some advice, that's all."

"There's enough money in the town fund to cover three squares and a flop—and maybe five dollars a day in wages."

Fargo sucked in his cheeks, mulling the proposition. The money was a pittance by gold-camp standards but not bad for a drifter who was temporarily unemployed because of Indian flare-ups.

While Fargo conned this over, he watched two women in fancy feathers, perhaps drawn by news of this latest bonanza, descend a staircase behind the long counter. Too well dressed to be sporting girls, he noticed, and with the prosperous swagger of madams. He had just started to study the busty redhead closer, trying to place her, when both women sang out in chorus: "Skye Fargo!"

They hustled down the steps and made a beeline to the counter.

"Skye Fargo, you handsome, hairy, dusty stallion!" the redhead greeted him, nuzzling his chest. "Remember Madame Larue's *maison* in the Barbary Coast?"

Fargo lifted his hat, swallowing her flattery without the least effort.

"Smooth Bore," he greeted the redhead, admiring her expensive velvet cape. "Tit Bit," he added, studying Smooth Bore's brunette younger sister. Fargo had tried to pry real names out of them once in San Francisco, but both women insisted those were the names history would know them by.

"Times must be mighty good for soiled doves," Fargo remarked. "Or you two are running the stable."

"We *own* the stable and this watering hole, too," Tit Bit said proudly, one finger tracing Fargo's chest muscles. "We sold Madame Larue's for a fortune."

She glanced at Jimmy, who was trying to act invisible. "You know how we know Skye, Marshal? See, he got a little feisty one night in Frisco and made a little bet with me and my sister— bragged he could please both of us at once or he'd pay double."

"And he *won* that bet, Jimmy," Smooth Bore cooed, blowing in Fargo's ear. "We were the high-class whores reserved for the high-stakes gamblers. But once that man climbs in the saddle, it's a fast gait and a long ride and *no* woman's letting go. Is that how you ride your women too?"

Jimmy took a desperate swig of beer and choked. "Jesus, lady, the mouth on you."

"You remember this sweet little rosebud mouth," she taunted him, "because it could be *on you* too. You're a handsome young stag."

Fargo laughed at Jimmy's boy-howdy confusion and watched while Tit Bit slid the silk-and-sequin fan from her décolletage. "I never seen a pecker like his," she blurted out to throw Jimmy deeper into a mill. "When I first seen it, I thought it was a war club. I—"

"You two girls tend to speak things that ought to just be thought," Fargo cut her off, almost as embarrassed as Jimmy. "Me and the marshal got some things to talk over."

"Oh, you'll see *us* later," Smooth Bore promised. "The two rooms at the top of the stairs are ours."

"But we'll only need one," Tit Bit reminded him.

"God's garters!" Jimmy swore after the two women flounced off to run the faro and monte games. "Those gals are what my ma called slatterns."

"Your ma used the right word. And Smooth Bore and Tit Bit

14

ain't whores with hearts of gold, either. But they're also tidy little bits of frippet."

"Oh, they're easy on the eyes," Jimmy conceded, adding slyly, "and, of course, if you were to hang around Virginia City a few days, you'd have easy access to both . . . ladies. Wha'd'ya say, Mr. Fargo?"

This place was a mare's nest, Fargo warned himself. He had made it a point to swing wide of mining towns as much as possible. He had once tangled with mining-camp vigilantes in the Black Hills, and he and his horse barely escaped alive. And now Terrible Jack Slade was in the mix, a man so dangerous that even his shadow could kill.

Fargo opened his mouth to decline Jimmy's offer. Just then his eyes again met the flat stone gaze of Nash Booth. This time, instead of looking away, his eyes bored aggressively into Fargo's. In a deliberate threat, he rested both palms on the butts of his shooters.

"I say you just hired yourself a roundsman," Fargo finally replied. "And it's clear to me there'll be plenty of *rounds* popping off."

Over the next hour several fistfights broke out in the saloon, quick as phosphors flaring up. But Fargo hardly noticed them—scratch a miner, the saying went, and you'll find a brawler.

"I only break them up," Jimmy explained, "when one man can't fight back. Otherwise the spectators will kill me—they place wagers on the outcome."

Fargo had expected trouble from Booth and his minions, but so far the night rider was holding his powder. But the Trailsman knew that when these experienced killers struck, it would be without warning.

"You know," Fargo remarked, nodding toward Booth's table, "from the profiteer's point of view, it's good to be shifty in a new country. A man grubbing for a fortune considers law a brake on his initiative."

"No offense, but that sounds close to criminal loving."

Fargo chuckled. "Nope, it's just understanding your enemy. Hell, you know that the lawless element is the majority on the Comstock. There's no law west of the Missouri River period except for a few overworked federal marshals like you. And we both know damn well you'll be plugged if you actually try to enforce any major laws."

"Sure as sunrise in the morning," Jimmy agreed. "Which leaves vigilantes and private vendettas to fill the gap."

Anticipating a frolic, Fargo had switched to beer—this local rotgut was brewed with strychnine and produced a crazy drunk. He watched Tit Bit and Smooth Bore crawling all over the already smashed prospector who had just struck color. Booth and his companions, too, kept glancing toward Gramlich with avid interest.

"Tell you what," Fargo said. "I think this prospector Bo Gramlich bears watching for his own protection. The way Booth has been glomming him like a cat on a rat tells me Bo will be 'persuaded' to sell out."

"He'll sell or he'll end up dinner for the hogs," Jimmy said. "And if he's killed my hands are tied because somehow witnesses don't exist around here. With no witnesses it's hard to even make an arrest. I can't hold a man simply on motive."

The young man trailed off, looking preoccupied with introspective doubts. "Skye? Jack Slade's midnight Wednesday threat— you think he's just taking us for a long sleigh ride?"

"Could be. He likes to pull off a good joke. We're dealing with a man who goes moon crazy at night, and then talks like a book and charms folks by day. I think *he* bears watching, too, at least at night."

Jimmy had been talking himself deeper and deeper into a slough of despondence. "All right, Skye, I'll get on his trail after sundown. But hell, this is Terrible Jack Slade and I'm just a normal man with no outstanding qualities like you got."

"Well, you'd better quit crying in your beer, sonny, and *find* some real quick, or both of us are going to die on the Comstock. T'hell with this farmer-boy humility and female hand-wringing, Marshal. Iowa is smoke behind you now. Pete says you enforced the law in Placerville, and you can enforce it here."

"Oh, I'll give it my damnedest. Us Helzers ain't quitters *or* cowards. But Placerville didn't pull in so many millionaires employing private armies of desperadoes."

"Speaking of desperadoes," Fargo muttered, "get your right hand under the counter and on your weapon. Here comes company."

Nash Booth crossed toward them, hands well away from his tied-down guns. Fargo thumbed his hat up to see the new arrival better. He had the lean and hungry look of a wolf on the hunt, and his dead button eyes sat atop a chiseled face scruffy with red gold beard stubble.

"Fargo," Booth greeted him in a civil tone, dismissing Jimmy with a glance. "Your reputation precedes you. My employer was so impressed to hear you're in town that he wants to talk to you. At your leisure, of course."

"Which employer?" Fargo asked without expression. "Septimus Dunwiddie or Ephraim Cole?"

Booth smirked. "'Pears to me that you been misinformed by the marshal. I only work for Cole. Hell, everybody knows that."

"Anyhow, thanks," Fargo said, "but I'm not looking for work."

"At least talk to him, man. The money is like having your own claim, only the work's easier. And it would be healthier for you than siding this sweet-lavender lawman. He's got rough weather ahead if he don't mend his ways."

Jimmy opened his mouth to make a retort to this clear threat, but Fargo sent him a quelling stare.

"Maybe I will palaver with Cole," Fargo said, "get the lay of the land. Tomorrow morning all right?"

"Jim dandy," Booth replied, lips twitching to hide his smugness. "I'll tell him to watch for you."

"I get it," Jimmy said after Booth went back to join his comrades. "You hire on with Cole and get the goods on this bunch from the inside."

Fargo shook his head. "Don't credit Booth's lies. No way in hell would he be eager to work with me. He prac'ly begged me to talk to Cole."

"Then why would Ephraim—"

"Good chance Cole *didn't* ask to see me or it's for another reason besides offering a job. And maybe Booth is just luring me onto his back forty for the kill."

"And you're *grinning* about it?"

Fargo looked pious. "Somebody's got to keep heaven packed with fresh souls."

He glanced toward the bunch at the table. "So Ephraim Cole hires this jasper Booth as head of security even *knowing* he's a hired gun for Dunwiddie?"

"Ephraim's a lawyer and probably knows how to protect his mine, which is awfully big to just up and steal like you might some creek-bottom diggings. Besides, I think Booth has him convinced the job for Dunwiddie is just a harmless sideline. Ephraim is not the hands-on type—he's always ciphering in ledgers."

"Fargo!" a gravelly voice said behind the Trailsman. "Finally I tracked you down, and now I'm gonna send you to glory, you wife-stealing son of a lowdown whore!"

A cap-and-ball pistol was cocked with a loud metallic *snick*. Fargo felt ice encase his spine as he realized the inevitable had caught up with him at last in the form of the pissed-off husband behind him. So this was the inglorious end of the trail?

"I suggest we talk about this, mister," Fargo said after swallowing hard.

"We'll *talk*, all right. About-face, you lanky bastard, so's the bullet is in the front all legal-like when I powder burn you. And *don't* go for that frogsticker in your boot. I know you're partial to it."

Fargo's mind began to form a plan even as he turned slowly away from the counter, expecting hot lead to perforate his liver at any moment.

"Howdy, Skye," a grinning old man in a slouch hat greeted him. "What's on your mind besides your hat?"

"Well, I'm a Dutchman! Snake River Dan, you're still above the horizon, you worthless sheep-humper? Last time I saw you was when we tangled with Swift Canoe's Cheyenne Dog Soldiers back at the Republican River."

Dan peered closely at Fargo's hat. "I see you done collected a couple new bullet holes in the crown of your conk cover. They oughter aim for your heart—hell, you ain't got a brain. You're all pecker, Fargo—a walking boner."

"Don't presume on those silver hairs," Fargo warned. "Old men splatter easy, but I *will* hit them. The hell you doing in a town like this, Dan? Towns were always 'cussed syphillization' to you."

"Ahh, the shining times is over boy—I been stall-fed too long," the old roadster confessed. "I've got lazy. Had me a nice cave just west of here in the foothills. Been running some traplines and selling long-fur pelts in Sacramento. But the Bannocks is on the scrap in that area, so this child lit a shuck for the settlements."

Jimmy was gawking at the old relic, so Snake River Dan directed his remarks to him. "Sprout, I done topped squaws with the best of the mountain men: the Sublettes, Carson, Bridger, Ogden . . ."

"You were a mountain man?"

Fargo suppressed a laugh as he took in the hawk-nosed old man with stringy silver hair. His pedigree as a "mountain man" was more lore than fact, but he was a fearless frontiersman who had survived plenty of scrapes. His skinny but sinewy arms were corded with veins, and a pair of Colt Dragoons was tucked into his red sash butts first for the quick cross draw.

"Was Snake River Dan a mountain man?" he repeated. "Tad, would a cow lick Lot's wife? Hell, I put up the first mileposts on the Oregon Trail just to help them peckerwoods out of my mountains. Back then Injins was just a damn nuisance, always begging and stealing. Now they'll gut any white man they catch alone taking a crap."

"Yeah," Fargo said, "but that's because at first they thought white people were just another small tribe breaking camp. Now they know they're being run out, so it's no surprise they've greased for war."

Snake River Dan looked skeptical. "The hell, Fargo? You done gone to the blanket—you flying their colors now?"

"The ass waggeth his ears. As a matter of survival I've killed more Indians than you'll ever see in all your nightmares. Anyhow, you're right about the gutting-a-white-man part. The warriors in these parts have rejected all treaties, and their medicine men are chanting the braves into a battle trance. If the war cry sounds, and enough tribes come together, it'll be a dirty business."

Fargo sent another glance toward Nash Booth and his henchmen. "But me and Jimmy have agreed that featherheads ain't the main threat in Virginia City—at the moment."

Snake River Dan also glanced toward the table. "Great jumpin' Judas, Fargo, you're at it again. I know *all* them scavenging curs, and, lad, I won't mince the matter. You ain't no man to take lightly, but Nash Booth was begot by fiends, and those egg-sucking varmints that side him are old hands at easy-go killing. I wouldn't mix into it. Just fork leather and light out."

"I'm in the mood for a little sport," Fargo replied.

"Hell, ain't none of your picnic, Skye. Me 'n' you has always roamed out beyond the settlements."

"Well, it's official now. Jimmy hired me on as a sort of sanitation engineer. I'll be helping him clean up the streets a little."

Snake River Dan, scowling, fished out his plug of black shag and sliced off a chaw with a clasp knife. He propped one elbow on the counter, cheeked the tobacco, and got it juicing good while he stared at Jimmy.

"Son," he demanded, "are you part of this brilliant plan?"

Jimmy nodded. "Evidently I'm the law around here."

"Well, I give you high marks for guts. But brains ain't your strong suit. Nash Booth would rape a nun and charge her for it. It'll be a holiday in hell before you two tame this snake den all by yourself."

"The way you say," Fargo agreed. "That's why you're going to help us."

Dan dismissed this obvious joke with a snort. "Ah, them newspaper stories about you, Fargo, don't signify. I won't swallow your bunk like some will."

"It's no bunk, Pop. I mean to get you killed."

Dan recognized Fargo's deadly serious tone and choked on his chewing tobacco. "Help? *This* child? Christ, I'd sooner lose a jaw tooth. 'Sides, my calves has gone to grass."

Fargo waved all this aside. "Snake River Dan is a name that's still feared between El Paso and the Canadian Rockies. I've seen you deal misery to Apaches, Comanches, and Mexican slavers. And old or not, you can lock horns with any owlhoot or paid thug in this town."

Fargo's lavish praise had done the trick just as he intended. Dan colored up like a bashful schoolgirl. "I *am* hell on two sticks, eh? Well . . . I'll have to study on it."

He glanced over at Booth's table, his beard-stubbled jaw firming. "These two-gun punks gripe my ass, all right. See that one in the cavalry hat, Willard Jones? That bastard shot my mule up near the Marias River. There's a reckoning due."

"Well, I'll be danged," Jimmy muttered, watching the batwings. "Skye, Booth's 'secret' employer just walked in. Take a gander at the pride of Baltimore, Septimus Dunwiddie, speculator."

3

"Christ on a crutch," Snake River Dan growled. "Ain't *she* pretty?"

Fargo watched an impressively barbered man dressed in gray broadcloth and fancy hand-tooled boots. He wore silver mutton-chops and a silk cravat with a diamond-headed pin. When he turned his head to survey the barroom, he presented a stiff profile like a cameo.

"That Dunwiddie needs to take him a good shit," Dan opined. "Stands like he's got an iron ramrod for a spine."

"And he's watching everything and everybody except Booth and his curly wolves," Fargo added. "That's real subtle, uh?"

Dunwiddie's eyes radiated exclusivity as he took in the common humanity around him. His gaze rested on Fargo. He seemed to be watching a wet mutt that had sneaked into his parlor.

"Here he comes," Fargo told his companions. "I'll deal with him. You two watch that table—this could be a distraction so they can plug us. If you see a hand disappear, shoot the whole bunch to doll stuffing."

Fargo turned sideways to monitor Dunwiddie. The speculator was freshly pomaded, brushed, powdered, and perfumed. He stopped close to Fargo and gazed at him silently, his face amused and patronizing, while he trimmed the end of a cigar with a cutter on his watch chain. He took in the dirty and bloody buckskins with cool distaste.

"Got a match . . . sir?" Dunwiddie asked, flashing a snide smile—and well aware the entire barroom was watching.

Fargo chuckled. He'd been down this trail before with rich but foolish men. Some felt they had to break every man to their will, a losing proposition in a world where there's always a better man.

Quicker than eyesight Fargo filled his fist. Dunwiddie's sa-

21

voir faire was suddenly impaired by the blue steel thrust into his testicles. Only Fargo's eyes grinned.

"Way I see it," he said in a dangerously pleasant tone, "this will cause you to sic your killers on me. That's hunky-dory with me. Saves me the trouble of hunting them down before I powder burn them. And then I'll settle accounts with you, poncy man."

Fargo tightened the pressure, pulling the hammer to half cock: a word no doubt on Dunwiddie's mind at the moment. A muscle near the speculator's mouth twitched violently.

"Don't even rowel me," Fargo said low in Dunwiddie's ear. "I got no tolerance for your kind, and I won't calibrate insults— you keep this plug-ugly shit up with me and I will gut you like a fish. That's the truth with the bark still on it. Now why don't you dust your hocks out of here, Suzy, and leave *men* to drink?"

Fargo lowered the hammer and leathered his Colt, watching Dunwiddie make a beeline for the doors.

"Hoss, that was a whizbang!" Snake River Dan declared after Dunwiddie rushed out. "I'll wager he's headed for a privy to clean his drawers."

"Skye, you were rough on him," Jimmy fretted. "This thing ain't over."

"That's the big idea, star man. I'm stirring up the shit so we can get this over pronto. Why drag it out when the numbers favor them?"

"Best way to cure a boil is to lance it," Dan agreed.

Fargo led his companions out onto the plank boards. "He-bear talk is cheap," he told Dan. "Are you ready for the hard sledding?"

"H'ar now! Don't fret none about *this* child. All's grist that comes to my mill."

Fargo's eyes studied the main street, which descended the west slope of Mount Davidson toward the diggings beyond the town limits. Something arrested his attention in an alley—pigs devouring a human body.

"That's the body I saw earlier," Fargo said. "I recognize the red plaid shirt."

"Best we can do," Jimmy said, his face troubled. "I can't keep up with the burying, and nobody wants the job."

Dan chuckled, unfazed by the grisly sight. "I say just leave the corpse for Terrible Jack Slade."

"You wanna spell that out?" Fargo said.

"All right: k-a-n-n-i-b-u-l-l. He's a goddamn cannibal, all right?"

"It's the latest rumor," Jimmy supplied. "Bodies *are* disappearing, and some claim Jack is eating them. But the truth is, the lousy sanitation in this town is more dangerous than cannibalism or Nash Booth. And so far it's taken more souls."

"I'll grant you all that," Fargo said. "But right now you're a lawman, not a politician. Keep your eye on the bead."

The lure of gold and silver brought a few men with all the accoutrements of wealth and upbringing. But it brought far more desperate pilgrims to the Comstock in droves. Fargo spotted a gaunt, half-dead man in tattered rags arrive pushing a wheelbarrow with all his worldly possessions in it: a sack of meal, a roll of blankets, and an old Hawken gun.

"Where you staying?" Fargo asked Snake River Dan.

"The onliest place with room left—Paddy Welch's Place. It's a miners' flophouse on Silver Street. Place is crawling with roaches and lice, and men are packed in like maggots in cheese."

"It'll do," Fargo said. "We'll be harder to kill in a crowded flophouse."

Dan's brow compressed with sudden anger. "That Dunwiddie! Fuck him with a crooked broomstick. Eastern money is the enemy of the westering man. Let's buck 'em *all* out in smoke."

"Sure, but rearguard actions won't get it done," Fargo warned. "We take the bull by the horns or we get gored."

"Man alive!" Dan froze mid step, staring out into the wide and dusty street. "*That* little piece hits you right bang in the eyes."

The little piece in question was a wasp-waisted beauty just then being handed out of a cabriolet by a well-armed man. Fargo took in her Scandinavian cheekbones and long brown hair in coronet braids. She wore a crisp white shirtwaist with a black wool skirt, but the modest clothing did little to suppress her swollen bodice and flaring hips.

"Well, now," Fargo said, "what have we here?"

Snake River Dan chuckled. "Fargo *does* love them fuzzies."

"I'd steer clear of her," Jimmy advised. "That's Loretta Perkins, and that's her permanent bodyguard with her. Her father is Luce Perkins, said to be a crackerjack mining engineer. He works for Ephraim Cole and the Schofield mine, which, if you credit the pub lore around here, is high on Septimus Dunwiddie's list of targets. That makes sense to me because Dunwiddie has been acquiring claims all around it."

"Future expansion," Fargo said, watching Loretta gather up some cloth from the conveyance. "These new 'consortiums' need to feed many hungry dogs or they go belly up. That means a giant operation going day and night. But say . . . I don't like it when a pretty girl is denied my company. That could stunt her growth. 'Scuse me, gents."

Fargo peeled away from his friends and stepped into the street. The guard, armed with two Colt Navy revolvers and a Spencer carbine, kept a wary eye on the man in buckskins.

"Good afternoon," Fargo greeted her. "You must be the prettiest nugget on the Comstock."

For a moment she glanced up from her remnants. Gunmetal eyes quick as lassos sized him up and then appeared to dismiss him.

"Step off, Jack," the guard warned.

Fargo ignored him. "It's just like taking medicine, isn't it?" he asked the young woman.

"What is?" she asked in a rich contralto voice.

"Giving me a smile."

She did indeed give him an inscrutable smile. "A woman who smiles at a man like you had better be ready for the consequences."

"Are you?"

"Am I what?"

"Ready for the consequences?"

The guard had lost all patience. He slid the carbine off his shoulder. "Mister, 'pears to me you're the third button on a two-button vest. Now light a shuck outta here or you've seen your last sunrise."

When Fargo ignored him, the guard drew his carbine back to smash it into Fargo's face. He easily blocked it with a muscular forearm, then dropped the man to his knees with a short, hard punch to the midsection. The guard's jaw went slack with stunned surprise and his face turned white as lard.

Fargo hauled back a fist to finish the job but realized Loretta was watching him. Not even the slightest flicker of an eyelid betrayed her true feelings at that moment. But she spoke in a tone of mild reproof. "My glory! Are you going to beat him to death in the street? That seems to be the preferred punishment in this barbaric place."

Fargo lifted the guard to his feet. "Looks like your rifle slipped, old son."

Knowing he'd overstepped, the guard nodded. "Yeah, but damn straight it won't slip again—not around you, mister."

Loretta paused to gaze into Fargo's eyes. "Lake blue. That's a promising augury," she said mysteriously as she turned toward a dressmaker's shop.

"What's an augury?" Jimmy asked as she retreated inside the shop.

Snake River Dan chuckled. "When *this* pussy hound is in the mix," he said, nodding toward Fargo, "it's a woman's cast-iron guarantee to give him a little slap 'n' tickle."

"Loretta Perkins? The Yellow River will run clear first," Jimmy insisted. "She likes opera and poetry and men who read some frog called Diderot. She's bound and determined to civilize this place. She even paid to stock and open a library."

"Yeah, I saw it," Fargo said. "It ain't exactly doing a land-office business."

"Ah, she's easy to look at, all right," Dan pitched in. "I felt my old peeder move when I seen them catheads swelling her shirt. But she's just another dumb frail. This child likes squeezing their tits, but stand 'em on their heads naked and they *all* need a shave."

"Spoken like a crusty old codger," Fargo said. "Boys, lead me to Paddy Welch's Place."

The moment Fargo rounded the corner onto Silver Street, a flash-pan filled with magnesia powder exploded.

"Dudley McCracken of the *Territorial Enterprise*," Jimmy explained. "Now every cockroach in the city will know you're here."

"That's jake by me," Fargo said. "I meant what I told Dunwiddie—it's easier to kill a man when he comes to you."

Paddy Welch's Place was a ramshackle frame structure serving as a sweat-reeking human warehouse. A dried cowhide sufficed as the main entrance. Some tumbledown furniture had been piled

25

into the corners to clear more floor space. Fargo planked his cash for the privilege of enough rough plank flooring to spread his blankets.

"It's a puke hole," Snake River Dan groused. "The jakes out back ain't but a straddle trench and there's no bathhouse. And this child don't cotton to breathing another man's farts."

Fargo shrugged as he shook out his bedroll. "A hungry dog must eat dirty pudding," he said cheerfully. "Any man who camps out in the desert will get his dander lifted. Hell, I once spent two days in a tree to avoid a Sioux war party."

Despite his chipper tone, Fargo studied the large room with misgiving. A lantern hanging from a crosstree of the ceiling, supplemented by a few tallow candles, cast an oily yellow light on the crowded room.

"I hope the kid don't aggravate Jack," Dan fretted. At sunset Jimmy had left to trail Slade. "That son of a bitch may be crazy, but he's smart as a steel trap."

Fargo nodded. "Sure he is, but the kid's a lawman—he can't be mollycoddled. Besides, I don't like Terrible Jack's prediction about how 'a beast will rise from the bowels of the earth'—and next Wednesday at midnight, to boot. Maybe it's just mad prophecy, but why the specific time and day?"

"That's a poser," Dan agreed.

"It's not just Jimmy—we've all got our dirty jobs," Fargo went on. "I'll be wet-nursing Bo Gramlich, and your job for now is to patrol—no, just wander through—the scattered prospectors' camps and the big shantytown at the foot of Center Street."

"And do what—shake my pizzle at the killers?"

"Why bother? They'd never see that limp slug. Just get a good look at any 'regulator' types—their horses, too. But don't try to brace anyone. You're just a blown-in old geezer on his way to bed. First we need to get our ducks in a row."

A man who worked twelve-hour shifts at the Dundee mine was already sound asleep next to Fargo, snoring with a racket like a boar in rut.

Dan snatched up his slouch hat and clapped it on, knees popping loudly as he pushed to his feet. "C'mon, there's an eating house next door. Happens I stay here, I'm gonna shoot that snoring bastard."

The tent-and-plank eating house had nothing left but sow-belly and corn bread, a meal Snake River Dan cheered. "On account of the warpath braves we're lucky to have it," he told Fargo. "All I've had for three days now is graveyard soup: milk and crumbled bread. Gives a man the squitters."

"Look," Fargo said, his tone impatient, "*all* food is bad out here right now. So bad, down at Fort Churchill, that the soldiers eat the corn meant for their horses. But you need to give over with this constant bellyaching and get your mind right. Old son, before this is over it's coming down to the nut-cuttin'."

As if to underscore Fargo's meaning, a man wearing the sturdy canvas trousers of a regulator stepped inside the hot, smoky tent. A Greener double-ten express gun rested in the crook of his left arm. His eyes slanted toward the long trestle table where Fargo and the old trapper were finishing their meal.

"Who you figure pays his wages?" Dan muttered.

"Prob'ly Dunwiddie since I had his pennies in a bunch earlier."

"Let's blast this skunk-bit coyote to trap bait—make it easier for Jack Slade to cook him."

Fargo chuckled. "You always were the boy for tossing dynamite at a gnat. He'll leave—he's just reporting on our whereabouts."

The paid gunsel left, and a few minutes later so did Fargo and Dan after a careful check past the tent flaps for ambushers. Seated again on their blankets at Paddy's, Dan used a curved horseshoe nail to scrape the black gunk from under his fingernails.

"J'ever wonder," he said slyly, "what it's like to get turned down by a woman?"

Fargo broke down his Henry and ran a wiping patch through the bore. "Not really. That's never been much of a problem for me."

"Ahuh. You *think* you're gonna play polish-the-picket-pin with that little Perkins filly, anh?"

"The thought crossed my mind."

"Ahuh. Wait'll you get in that fancy parlor of hers and drink your coffee from the saucer like the rube you are. She's too silky satin for your rough hide."

"How would you know that?"

27

"All's grist that comes to my mill, remember? This child has heard plenty about Loretta Perkins. She ain't like your usual frontier consorts. She don't trade off her favors for whatever she needs like most of the females in these diggings."

Fargo grinned. "All women are alike under their petticoats, hoss. They have a terrible itch, and I'm there to scratch it. You best check for powder clumps—we'll be heading out soon."

Dan gave up with a sigh. "Reckon I can't strike a spark where there ain't no flint. Blast! I never figured I could bend to settlement ways. I should be a day's ride west of here walking my traplines. My last bed was a heap of sweet-smellin' spruce boughs, and that air in the Sierras is a reg'lar tonic."

This talk of fresh air made Dan pause and sample the air with his nose. Fargo, too, smelled the sour stench of fermenting vinegar.

"Fritz!" Dan barked out. "Haul that skunk den outside!"

"*Ja, ja,* kiss *mein* ass," the German miner called back, refusing to part with his beloved sauerkraut keg.

"Ease off," Fargo warned his friend. "This is what I mean about you. Don't worry. You'll see plenty of fighting in this wide-open heller."

Sitting cross-legged on the hard floor, Fargo unleathered his belt gun. He set the single-action Colt's hammer at half cock and palmed the wheel to check the action. Suddenly a grin parted his lips.

"You should've seen Jimmy earlier," he said. "The lad had a little shock with Smooth Bore. You know that stable-sergeant mouth on her. She gave the marshal a little of her bedroom sass, and he blushed to his earlobes."

"He can kiss his hinder good-bye happens she sets her cap for him—her *night*cap."

"Jimmy's a stout lad," Fargo said, "but he's trying to stop the lawless element with arrests and indictments—but when witnesses refuse to cooperate only summary justice can work."

"He's trying to stuff the hog by way of its ass," Dan agreed. "But say! Glom this."

Dan pulled a well-preserved rattlesnake hide from his poke. "This here might be good for a hoot. I know Pete Helzer, Jimmy's brother. Did he tell you the kid's got a God-fear of rattlesnakes?"

Fargo grinned. "I take your drift. But right now we best ride out and give him a hand. I noticed today how Booth and the others looked right through Jimmy—like he's already dead. C'mon, let's make tracks."

Their eyes constantly scanning the steep, lumber-denuded terrain of Virginia City, the two men rode shank's mare to the livery and whistled in their horses from the paddock. Snake River Dan, who despised a pretty horse as weak, had acquired a dish-faced skewbald so ugly that the Ovaro shied back at first meeting uncertain what manner of creature this was.

Both men tacked their mounts. "You know what to do," Fargo said. "Be careful now at all times and keep your eyes to all sides. I sent out the first soldier when I put the crusher on Dunwiddie's oysters, and now we're all marked. Either we put the kibosh on them or they rabbit from these parts—no third way."

Fargo stepped into leather and swung up and over, shaking out the reins. "I'll ride out first. See you back at Paddy's."

Just before Fargo and the Ovaro were swallowed by the shape-shifting darkness, Dan called out behind him, "Luck to you, Fargo."

Fargo was long familiar with the degradation of human nature under adversity, and the degradation in Virginia City was well advanced. Merely propping up a wagon tongue made a hanging easy. Dead bodies were devoured by pigs, imported thugs operated openly, and the debased population would not fight back.

Despite the incredible wealth being mined, many men lived in dire poverty and had no strength to fight back. The stark contrast in wealth staggered Fargo. There were a few men on the Comstock so rich they could equal the wealth of entire cities and states, and many more were so poor they rolled their tobacco in cornhusks.

He let the Ovaro set his own pace on Center Street, sticking to an apron of shadow and swinging wide of the few streetlamps that kept the street from pitch blackness. More light spilled from the endless strip of saloons, gambling houses, whorehouses, dancehalls, and "theaters," most of the latter supplying crude fare that would make a mule blush.

Fargo reined in close to the Wicked Sisters and lit down, standing behind the shoulder of his stallion to watch the batwings. He knew that Bo Gramlich had been celebrating hard, and with luck the prospector might be winding down soon.

"Skye! Skye Fargo! I'm over here . . ."

Fargo followed the sound of the female voice back to an upstairs window of the Gold Room across the street. It was one of the girls he'd seen running naked in the street earlier.

"Howdy, Mr. Buckskins! It's Trudy again. Stop by anytime. The line can wait."

Fargo doffed his hat, relieved when a brawny male arm pulled her from the window. From inside the Wicked Sisters he recognized the drunken voice of Gramlich rising above the din: "Hell, I just might get married. A man can't blame *everything* on the government."

Fargo heard boot heels thumping on the plank walk. He pretended to adjust the throatlatch on the Ovaro's bridle.

"The hell you doing here, mister—playing with yourself?"

Fargo glanced at a standard-issue boomtown thug, probably imported by one of the mines to watch for outside agitators who might organize labor strikes. A swath of lamplight traced the shadowy crags of his face.

"I asked you a question, shit heel. The hell you doing here?"

Fargo stepped into the weak light. "Look that question up in the almanac, back shooter."

Fargo's Colt sprang into his fist and he thumb cocked it. The hired gun stared at the steeled features of a face used to domination.

"Everything alive has the right to go on living," Fargo said, "until it tries to take that right from me."

"You," the man said. "Hell, I didn't try—"

"Shut your filthy sewer and heed my words. I'm working with the marshal now, only I don't have his . . . legal limitations. I will kill every vigilante, night rider, and crooked mine owner I have to, but law *is* coming to Virginia City. Spread the word."

Fargo planted a boot in the man's chest and sent him sprawling. He sprang to his feet and scurried off without looking back.

Ten minutes later, Bo Gramlich staggered out of the saloon. Weaving precariously, he headed down the steep grade that led to the mines and claims as well as the shantytown for mine workers and a few isolated prospectors' camps. Fargo knew that Center Street petered out at a gulch below, a dead-end canyon.

He played a hunch and didn't follow Gramlich right away. Sure enough, a few minutes behind Gramlich came Sam Watson and Chilly Davis, two of the "private police" who'd been at Nash Booth's table.

Leading the Ovaro, Fargo stayed well back and watched the two catch up to Gramlich. There was a great deal of joviality and backslapping, and soon one of the night riders had produced a bottle of cheap redeye, foisting it on Gramlich.

The trio, all singing bawdy choruses about Lu-lu Girl, reached a clump of tents and mud hovels located behind a huge mound of ore tailings. They stepped past the fly of a tent and Fargo watched a lantern glow to life from within. He threw the Ovaro's reins forward to hold him in place and slipped up to the entrance.

Gramlich sat on a hidebound trunk, so drunk his face was red and bloated. Sam Watson, a fat but powerful-looking man, produced a sheaf of papers from the inside pocket of his rawhide vest. "Here you go, Bo. Here's that paper we drew up for you. You sign that little puppy and we'll give you five thousand dollars, cash on the barrelhead."

"Hell, think of it, Bo," threw in Chilly Davis. "That's gold you don't gotta pull out of the ground. Easy money."

"Easy money," Gramlich repeated, barely able to sit upright. "Mighty kind of you fellows. Lemme sign it."

"Sorry to spoil your big time, boys," Fargo announced, stepping inside the rancid-smelling tent. "The ratcatcher is here."

Davis tried to aim his double ten, but Fargo's Henry came to the level first. "Try that again and you'll fry everlasting."

"So what's scratchin' at you, mister?" Watson demanded belligerently.

"This," Fargo replied, snatching the paper from Gramlich and quickly perusing it.

"That's legal," Watson insisted. "You got no right to queer the deal."

"This is enlightening," Fargo said. "This 'contract' isn't in the name of Septimus Dunwiddie or Ephraim Cole. So you boys are stealing Bo's claim all for yourselves. Plan on being a bunch of big bugs, huh?"

"Stealing?" Davis protested. "Fargo, this play ain't crooked. Hell, we give you our word—"

"Your *word* ain't worth a busted trace chain."

"Fargo," Watson said, "you ain't a miner, so you don't know how these big strikes work. Long before you come here, me and the boys started a claims cooperative to protect—"

"Sure, sure," Fargo cut him off impatiently, "all this happened long before once-upon-a-time, right?"

"Hunh?" Watson's flesh-folded face clouded with anger. "You calling us liars?"

"Give the fat man a cigar. I sure's hell ain't calling you scrubbed angels. You weasel-dick scrotes wouldn't know the truth if it mule-kicked you. If Bo hadn't agreed to sign this jack-leg contract for you, you two yellow curs would have killed him and forged his name—it's likely an 'X' anyway."

Fargo tore the paper to shreds. "You been warned because I'm in a generous mood tonight. Try this grift again and you'll be picking lead out of your livers."

Fargo racked a bullet into the chamber of his Henry. "Matter fact, I'm thinking maybe you two should leave for a healthier climate. A lot of colic will soon be going around—lead colic."

Watson purpled with rage. "Eat shit, you arrogant son of a bitch! Ain't no mother-loving crusader coming to *our* diggings and ordering us out. Fargo, you'll soon be feeding the hogs."

Fargo knew this criminal type well. They had some ambition but lacked the intelligence needed to translate ambition into action. So they licked the fingers of smarter men. And though these lickfingers could never be better men, Fargo intended to make them wiser. So the moment Watson finished his threat, Fargo delivered a powerful roundhouse right that rocked Watson sideways and sent his eyes rolling up. Fargo followed with a crushing uppercut that lifted the big man's heels off the ground before dropping him in an unconscious heap.

Chilly Davis backed away, holding out imploring hands. "I didn't give you no sass, Mr. Fargo."

"No, so I won't touch you—tonight. But if I see you two flies buzzing around here again, I'll kill you for cause. And before I do, I'll whip you until hell won't have it again."

A tired and sleepy Fargo retrieved his stallion and made the half-mile ride up the slope of Mount Davidson. It must have been around midnight, Fargo guessed, but Virginia City had the steady roar of a boomtown so rich that Congress feared it might someday take over the United States.

He quickly rubbed down the Ovaro with an empty flour sack and then turned him out into the paddock after forking some hat into the net. Fargo returned to the flophouse in Silver Street and picked his way carefully through the sleeping men. Snake River Dan, too, had just returned and was pulling off his knee-length moccasins when Fargo arrived.

"You smell like quiff," Dan greeted him in a hoarse whisper. "You spent all this time diddlin' Loretta Perkins steada gelding bullyboys, dint'cha?"

"Shush it," Fargo told the old gas pipe, unbuckling his shell belt. He hadn't slept two hours straight for a week now, and his eyelids felt weighted with coins. "We now have clear title to hell, old son. But for tonight I plan to sleep peacefully and let the future take care of itself."

4

Fargo enjoyed the sleep of the just until the shrill scream of the six a.m. whistles called miners to their stopes and drifts.

Snake River Dan was tying on his red sash. "Fargo," he greeted the newly wakened man, "didja powder burn a curly wolf or two last night?"

Fargo scowled. He pulled a hundred-count carton of self-contained handgun cartridges from his saddlebag. "You and your damn lust for gunplay. Me, I generally try to talk my way out of a shooting scrape. Sometimes I get a box with no misfires. Other times up to half a box fails with this new factory-pressed ammo."

"It's your own damn fault, hair face. You wouldn't stick to the old ways. These newfangled repeaters ain't worth a kiss-my-ass."

Dan cupped his hands around his mouth and raised his gruff voice to a shout: "Well, we're all just merrier than mice in a bakery, hey? Drop your cocks and grab your socks—it's another glorious day on the Comstock!"

"Pipe down, dad!"

"Put a stopper on your gob, you soft-brained fool!"

A chorus of curses and groans, punctuated by a few death threats, made Dan slyly chuckle. "This child likes to spread a little joy everyplace he goes."

"Yeah, just like you used to spread your seed at every Indian camp. Listen, how'd it go last night?"

"I done what you told me. Wandered around the shantytown and the prospectors' camps. Saw a teamster beat to death with pick handles. I got a good size-up of a few night riders and their horses."

"Good. We'll scratch it down on paper later. I want names, too."

Fargo gazed around the big room, watching hardworking, desperate men prepare for another brutal day's labor. Most looked stoic but hopeless, some having gone bust as prospectors.

"Dan, you were right yesterday," Fargo remarked as he slid his Arkansas toothpick into its boot sheath. "Both of us should just ride out. But we won't."

Dan looked puzzled. "Hell's bells, chumley, why not? We done earned our laurels and to spare. We've counted coup on Injins from every warring tribe west of the Big Muddy and some from east of it. We've locked horns with Mex bandits, Comancheros, vigilantes, freebooters—ain't our fault Jimmy was stupid enough to take the federal oath."

"You can ride on," Fargo said. "I'm sticking."

"Ahuh. On account you got you some juicy cunny lined up. Smooth Bore, Tit Bit, and the Perkins gal for dessert."

"That's the only real entertainment," Fargo admitted, "but the order I take them in doesn't matter. The other reasons don't require talking about."

"That's your usual line of blather when you want to get my life over. Fargo, you pigheaded son of a bitch. Well, then, reckon I'll die in Virginia City."

"Not me—I'm damned if I'll end up as pig dung. C'mon—Jimmy's meeting us at the eating house."

Fargo stood behind the cowhide flap and surveyed Silver Street well before emerging from Paddy's flophouse. Despite the early hour a sky as pure and perfect and flawless as blue china domed the vast territory. The soft green foothills of the Sierra range curtain-folded upward on Fargo's left, while the brutal desert glare to the north marked ill-fated Pyramid Lake and the sterile deserts that left much of Nevada Territory an unexplored frontier controlled by warpath Indians.

Jimmy was waiting for them at the crude eating establishment. A chunk of cold pone, and a cup of even colder coffee, had to suffice for Fargo's breakfast.

"I kept an eye on Slade last night," Jimmy reported. "But from a safe distance."

Fargo approved this with a nod. "You don't want to close-herd Terrible Jack. See anything suspicious?"

"Nah. He didn't get plowed last night, so he didn't go wild. One thing, though—there was a dead body on San Francisco

35

Street, throat slashed. Last night Jack studied it for a long time. This morning when I sent the undertaker it was gone. And the pigs don't wander in that area."

Fargo and Snake River Dan exchanged glances.

"Fargo," Dan said, "you and me both know that in starving times people is sometimes et. This child has got no stomach for it, but I seen corpses standing in for vittles one hard winter in La Glorieta Pass. But Jack? The food ain't fancy around here, least-ways not lately, and you'll notice there's no stray dogs, but he sure's hell ain't starving."

"No," Fargo agreed, "if he's eating corpse flesh it's because he's full-blown crazy."

"You two can have him," Snake River Dan said. "That Willard Jones is mine. Bastard killed the best mule I ever had."

"Terrible Jack is crazy, and crazy men are bad medicine," Fargo said. "We just need to make sure his midnight-next-Wednesday threat is more crazy talk. I wouldn't lay long odds, though, that it is."

Fargo watched the door as he spoke. "Jack's just part of it. When things come to a head around here, we could use a few more friendlies on our side. Jimmy, your brother told me there was a twelve-man cavalry squad stationed here."

"There was. But their mustang lieutenant spent all day making them do full-pack drill in the hot sun—punishment for drunkenness and sloth. He was found shot through the head and genitals, and his men scattered to the four directions."

Fargo nodded. "No wonder the pond scum in all these boom-towns find it so easy to take over."

"Sam Watson and Chilly Davis," Jimmy said, "the two you rousted last night, ain't been here long. Dame Rumor says they were holed up somewhere in the Red Wall, that giant sandstone ridge way east of here."

Fargo nodded. "It may be a long way from here, but I know that ridge. It's chock-full of hidey-holes for the worst killers in the West. If those two roosted there, then count on it—Booth is hiring the best of the worst. Well, in a little bit I'll have my meeting with Ephraim Cole, and I should have a better idea whether he's jobbing out the killing."

"Happens there really *is* a meeting," Snake River Dan reminded him. "Booth mighta laid a trap for you."

"He's trapped and killed others," Jimmy chimed in, "though of course I can't prove it."

"Gets a man's blood singing," Fargo said cheerfully. "Deception, death . . . hell, I feel blessed."

"Fargo, you're moonstruck," Dan opined, chuckling.

Jimmy squinted at Fargo as if wondering about his sanity. "You'll find Cole at his 'field office' in the back of the assay shack at the Schofield."

Outside, Fargo parted from his companions and walked to the livery at the east end of Center Street. After letting the Ovaro shake out the night kinks, Fargo tossed on blanket, pad, and saddle, then snugged the bridle and swung up onto the hurricane deck. Center Street was crowded with rides and conveyances, and Fargo tried to stay inconspicuous. Assassination, in outlaw hellholes like this, would be news for one day at most.

He let the Ovaro set his own pace heading down the slope of the mountain, growing more vigilant as they slowly clopped past the smelting house for the Schofield mine, ore heaped about in conical piles. The smelters produced thick billows of black smoke that left a coating of soot on everything in town. When Fargo rode through the blast-furnace heat, it evaporated the moisture on his eyeballs.

He spotted the assay shack not far from the headframe marking the main entrance to the mine. He reined in among a clutch of juniper bushes, making sure his horse was hidden from the road. Then he struck out on foot across the scarred and ruined terrain, head swinging left and right as he watched for attackers.

Fargo spotted no one but an isolated Chinese worker sifting through ore tailings and a skip operator clanging his bell before plunging down into the earth with another load of miners. Fargo began to wonder if his little visit last night with Watson and Davis had given Nash Booth pause.

At first, when Fargo glimpsed a flickering, twirling reflection in the corner of his right eye, he guessed it was only sunlight glinting off an exposed gold vein. But the hurtling brightness grew rapidly closer, and his muscles grasped the truth before his mind could. Fargo saw it reach its top arc and start to fall toward him. A glass bottle filled with a waxy yellowish liquid.

A squiggle of prickling current shot along his spine. *Unstable nitro*, Fargo thought, his skin going cold as ice. If he hunkered down it would land dangerously close. His only thought was to get clear of that deadly explosive.

Tossing his Henry out ahead of him, Fargo did a deep knee bend and then gave a powerful leap, landing in a deliberate tumble and rolling headlong. A cracking explosion just behind him shook the ground as dirt, rocks, and clumps of dried mud slapped in all around him. A chunk of debris caromed into the back of his left ankle and left it sore and throbbing.

"Hey, mister!" shouted a skip operator. "You all right?"

Fargo nodded, gingerly pushing to his feet. An explosion, on the busy Comstock Lode, hardly merited notice, and outside of the skip operator no one appeared to have seen it. Fargo revolved slowly around but spotted no one. Heaps of ore and tailings everywhere supplied perfect cover for any ambushers.

Limping slightly, Fargo retrieved his rifle and headed for a door at the back of the assay shack. It already stood open, and a man peered out at him quizzically over a pair of gold-rim spectacles.

"Skye Fargo, I presume?"

"In the flesh—just barely. And you're Ephraim Cole?"

The man nodded, moving aside so Fargo could enter. Fargo's first glimpse of Cole put him in mind of the phrase "a man more important than meritorious." A long gray duster protected his suit, and the hand-stitched and tooled boots had to cost more than one of his miners made in three months. A long mane of flowing silver hair gave him the appearance of a wealthy prophet.

"Your boys gave me a sweet reception out there," Fargo said, peering around at the leather-bound account ledgers stacked everywhere.

"Fargo, you have no proof it was any of my employees. But even if it was, *I* had nothing to do with it. I'm the last one to want you dead—I'm hoping to hire you."

"I'm a popular man around here," Fargo said in a sarcastic tone.

Cole began pacing up and down the office, his pale face flushed with the urgency of a man on a mission. "Fargo, I wouldn't expect a frontier rustic like you to understand this, but huge forces are at work. Providence is operating on a grand scale to accomplish its designs. It is our manifest destiny, sir, to fulfill God's will and conquer this wild continent. We cannot fail because God favors the white race. Rain will follow the plow even in the deserts. Once the red vermin are exterminated we will enjoy the milk and honey."

Fargo burst out laughing. "Serve it on toast, why'n'cha? I guess once a man turns his greed into a religious destiny, he can also turn shit into strawberries."

"Greed is good, Fargo, and perfectly legal. I'm an attorney—you'll find no flies on me. I take every advantage of the law, yes, but do not break it."

"Does that hold for the men you employ for security?"

"Nash Booth and his comrades are no hallowed saints, granted. But, Fargo, there's a million dollars in loose gold lying around these big mines. And miners are ingenious at smuggling it out—they even spread tar on their shoes to pick up the nuggets. But Nash and his crew do a good job of stopping all that. Every day they save me much more than I pay them."

Fargo grimaced at a twinge of pain in his swelling left ankle. "All right, suit yourself. But Booth and his cronies are *not* loyal to the brand. You took a viper to your breast when you hired those killers, and it will sink fangs into you. There's a rumor that Nash also works for Septimus Dunwiddie, so it's possible that your model worker is helping to steal your mine."

Cole tugged a handkerchief from his breast pocket and patted his forehead.

"I know that," he confessed. "I'm scared to death of Nash. Oh, he pretends I'm his boss, but nobody controls him. That's why I need to hire you. Nobody else in this city can stop him."

"I've got a job," Fargo said. "And the two might conflict."

"You've *got* to help me, Fargo. I was already being pecked to death by a thousand baby chicks and now the carrion birds are circling. Name your price."

Fargo shook his head. "Booth and the rest have killed innocent men and rooked others out of their claims. Maybe you didn't order them to do it, but you have to know it's going on."

Cole shrugged as if disclaiming any blame. "I run an honest mine. It's Dunwiddie who resorts to crimes. How about fifty dollars a day?"

The offer staggered Fargo, but he showed no reaction. "I don't chew my cabbage twice, Mr. Cole."

"You thirst for a mirage, you fool! The world will never grow honest."

For some men, Fargo realized, money was a bludgeon. This blustering lawyer was helpless without it.

"It's because I'm one of the rich sons of bitches—is that it, Fargo? You've never had a pot to piss in nor a window to throw it out, and you hate my stinking guts for being wealthy?"

Fargo headed for the door and paused with one hand on the latch. "Wealth is fine if it's made more or less honestly and doesn't make a whore of a man's soul."

Cole's fleshy, feminine lips pursed into a sneer. "You a preacher now?"

Fargo's brow darkened. "Yeah—in the Church of Righteous Vindication."

The warning in his tone calmed Cole down. But he lodged one last plea. "Everyone knows your reputation. But you're vastly outnumbered here. Why fly in the face of destiny? Some of my workers are military veterans, you can—"

"Save it for your memoirs," Fargo cut him off. "Far as Nash Booth and his curs—you and me have a shared interest there, and you might get what you want without hiring me. After this nitro attack just now, I see how it is—I'm going to have to kill that bunch."

Favoring his sore leg, Fargo returned to his stallion. A little smoke still hazed the spot where the nitro exploded. He led the Ovaro out to the freight road and was about to hit leather when a musical female voice arrested him. "Mr. Fargo? Yoo-hoo, Mr. Fargo!"

Fargo glanced to his right and spotted a little grassy dell he'd missed before. Willow trees formed a private room around it. Fargo was pleasantly surprised to see Loretta Perkins striding toward him, looking fetching in a white muslin dress set off by a blue sash tied tight to emphasize her tiny waist. Her gaily beribboned hat was fastened with a six-inch pin.

Fargo quickly speared his fingers through his hair and dusted off his hat. "You look pretty as four aces, Miss Perkins," he greeted her.

She gave him a hesitant one-sided smile, as if not sure whether genteel ladies should talk to his type. "The explosion . . . Father and I heard it. Are you all right? I see you're limping."

"Stone in my boot," Fargo replied, "although I'm flattered by your concern."

His lake blue eyes savored this haughty beauty. "You're strolling around alone in some dangerous real estate, aren't you?"

"I'm not alone. My father is here with me. Now and then I bring him a bottle of tea. We drink it together here while I read to him."

"I have to admit this is about the only peaceful-looking spot I've seen in the area. Still, this is no place for a woman."

Red spots flared in her delicately sculpted cheeks. "*Merci mille fois.* A thousand thanks for such original advice. I should have known the newspapers would lie about your true nature."

"It's even more flattering to know you follow my exploits," Fargo goaded in a tone of exaggerated innocence. "If you'd like a memento—"

"How *dare* you? I simply saw the latest newspaper broadsheets, which you probably paid to have written—certainly a rustic like you can't write."

"I am a simpleton, yes, but I do a few things exceedingly well," Fargo assured her. "And one of them I aim to do with you."

Her color heightened noticeably. "You vulgar boor! I am engaged to Lucian Martin Pendergast, Esquire, prominent Boston lawyer. No sensible woman cuckolds Hyperion for a low satyr."

"Well, now. I have no idea what you just said. But such highhanded carrying-on is likely to put you on my mind—exactly where you want to be, I'd wager. Day and night—especially night."

She became so angry at him that her long-lashed eyelids quivered. "I suppose your barracks-room 'wit' appeals to the gallery. You, sir, are an outrage to femininity. Luckily you'll find plenty of women here to match your low breeding."

"Until we meet again," Fargo said as she started to turn away. His words stopped her.

"Meet again? I, speak to a brute like you? The unmitigated gall!"

He laughed. "Lady, your mind takes more turns than a crosseyed cow. Who started *this* conversation?"

Again red spots leaped into her cheeks. "I . . . Well, they'll make cheese out of chalk before I do it again!"

Fargo watched her storm off in high dudgeon, a grin spreading inside his beard. "That did it," he told his stallion. "She hates me. It's easy pickings now."

Fargo forked leather and shook out the reins. He gigged up his horse and began the long ascent up the mountain slope to town. Soon, however, he had to rein out of the way to let a freight caravan pass. The packhorses were down-headed and dragging their feet, forcing the drivers to shout, "Hep! Hep!" in a bellowing roar and crack their long blacksnake whips furiously over the horses.

Seeing the packtrain prompted Fargo to ride on through town and down the eastern slope of Mount Davidson. He continued on past the little trickle stream known as Smoke Creek, where a low ridge provided a good view to all sides. He took a good squint in every direction, finding the brownish yellow terrain sparse of growth except for the small oasis of Silver Springs. Farther out the desert turned a burning white under shimmering heat waves.

Only Death Valley and the Salt Desert of Utah could match this desolate view in Fargo's experience. The trained eye of a lifelong trailsman and scout read nothing alarming until he searched the northeast horizon toward the huge Great Basin at the heart of Nevada Territory. Now and then a bright flash caught Fargo's eye—flashes that could well be made by mirrors or the silver conchos so valued by the far-western tribes.

For weeks now, while riding between Sacramento and Fort Churchill, Fargo had noticed the moccasin telegraph was highly active: smoke, mirror flashes, even runners. But despite his long efforts he had never succeeded in cracking any tribe's signals, and he had no way to know what was in the cards. Fargo knew one thing, however: despite all the firepower in Virginia City, this unorganized collection of drunkards was vulnerable to well-timed Indian attacks.

Fargo returned to the livery and rubbed down the Ovaro, combing the witch's bridles out of its mane before filling the wooden water trough. As he neared the Wicked Sisters saloon he was reminded that a bonanza drew all kinds—a small crowd had gathered around to mock a bluestocking from some enlightened commune back in the States called Brook Farm.

She exhorted everyone to give up the quest for "filthy Mammon" and to spend their days farming and baking bread—this to heal their "dwarfed and mutilated souls." Fargo took in the reformer's horse face and lantern jaw and hoped *her* soul was in better repair than its mortal shell.

He found the saloon only a third full. Fargo searched for unfriendly faces, spotting Nash Booth and Willard Jones at a center table. Both men pretended not to see him. He also spotted Snake River Dan sitting at a table with his back to a wall, scowling into a jolt glass.

"What are you searching for in that glass?" Fargo greeted him. "Your lost teeth?"

"I'll pop you on your snot locker, Fargo. I figured you was gone beaver by now."

"Brother, you laid good odds. The Grim Reaper tickled my ribs about an hour ago."

"That close, uh?"

"A few feet closer," Fargo assured him, "and I'd be deader than a dried herring."

He sent quick glances toward Booth and Jones as he explained about the assassination attempt and his brief talk with Ephraim Cole, owner of the Schofield.

"Look at them lily-livered mange pots," Dan said, scowling darkly toward Booth and Jones. "Scairt to even look at you. That Willard Jones is up from deep Texas. Word has it he run a white-slave ring out of El Paso until the Rangers run him out."

Fargo turned the problem of that morning's attack back and forth in his mind. "You know, there's no proof yet that Nash or his toadies did it."

"Proof!" Dan farted with his lips. "There's no *proof* I'll live out this day, neither, but I ain't diggin' no damn grave. A man requires no proof that he's been bit hard in the ass."

Fargo grinned. "That fossil you call a brain strikes a lode now and then."

"Ahuh, and here's another nugget for you, lover boy: Smooth Bore and Tit Bit got definite plans for you. Take a gander at the game tables."

Fargo did. Monte and faro, being fast and reckless games of chance, were more popular than poker among boomers. One sister ran each game: Smooth Bore the faro rig, Tit Bit the monte cards. The moment Fargo glanced their way, both women sent him searing gazes before pointing up toward their rooms.

"Need anything, Mr. Fargo?" Tim Bowman called from behind the counter, trying to look discreet.

"Just two barley pops," Fargo said. "And draw one nappy."

"T'hell with that temperance tea," Dan erupted. "Let's fling one, Fargo. This child ain't been on a jollification since Christ was a corporal."

"Have you been visiting the peyote soldiers? This is no time or place to skylark. That's the one mistake these puke pails are waiting for. You *will* temper your drinking."

"Pitch it to hell," Dan snapped, his weathered face sour and spiteful. "You can take this whole goddamn town and bury it in fish guts for aught I care. Why the hell do we need gold anyhow? Swapping goods and services works fine, and no slick-talkin' bankers is needed. Gold makes men so rich they can shit on the law."

Fargo nodded as he tasted the flat beer. "That shines. And from what I've seen, the most accomplished thieves and scoundrels are the eagle screamers like Cole who wear the flag for a mask. They can turn outright crimes into patriotic flapdoodle like manifest destiny."

Dan's wild gray eyebrows formed a bushy "V." "Manifest whosis?"

"Never mind. We got company."

Smooth Bore stopped behind Fargo's chair, trailing a scent of jasmine, and digging a hand so deep into his hair that his hat fell off.

"Hey, there, longshanks," she cooed in his ear, her breath soft and warm. "Me and Tit Bit wonder if you couldn't . . . stop by later to visit us."

Fargo felt the busty redhead's endowment pressing into his neck. He glanced toward the monte table. Tit Bit, her shiny brunette hair cascading loose over her shoulders, sent him a wink.

"Us?" Fargo repeated. "You mean both of you . . . at once?"

"Of course, goose. Just like in San Francisco. You liked it then, didn't you?"

"Naturally. I did my best, but either one of you girls alone is a challenge."

"You done real good," she assured him, hot-licking his ear. "That's why we need it again. Abyssinia later, all right?"

"Katy Christ, Fargo," Dan teased him after Smooth Bore

44

sashayed back to the faro table, "ain't it enough that you screw every woman you see? Now you hafta schedule 'em in pairs. You ain't the Trailsman—you're the Cocksman."

"I've been called worse. Say, here comes Jimmy, and that lad looks like somebody kicked his dog."

The marshal dropped into the third chair and expelled a long sigh. "Gents, it's a lunatic's holiday out there. Word of Jack Slade's midnight-next-Wednesday threat has spread all over town. Most think it's all just air pudding. A few calamity howlers fear the town will be leveled."

"I'd keep watching him nights," Fargo advised. "He's trickier than a redheaded woman."

"Smooth Bore's a redhead," Dan reminded him.

"You just made my point."

Fargo brought Jimmy up to date on events earlier at the mine. "You said there's no proof Cole is breaking the law, and maybe that's so. But trying to sort his actions out from Booth's is like trying to separate the water from the wet."

"Lookit them dick weevils," Dan said, staring at the two night riders and spoiling for a fight. "Peace-piping won't get 'er done, boys. They figure we'll get chicken guts now. Either we put the crusher on 'em quick or they curl our toes for us."

Fargo thumbed foam off his mustache. "You're right, old campaigner, but I'm thinking we underrated the Indian threat. I think I saw signs today that they're watching Virginia City. It's hard to say what that means, but they are hopping mad that white men are taking the glittering yellow rocks from what they consider their land."

"But you said Indians don't attack towns this size," Jimmy pointed out.

"It's true that most Indian braves won't ki-yi their ponies in a massed attack on a place this built up. But they have been known to sneak into towns at night to plant fire bundles. Then they withdraw and ignite the bundles with flaming arrows. And with this town so close-built, it would go up like a powder keg."

Snake River Dan nodded. "God's own truth. They've burned settlers out of the New Mexico Territory and south Texas."

Jimmy looked crestfallen. "Hell and damnation! Talk about piling on the agony. Saving this town from Indians is the army's job. It's U.S. territory."

"Give the infant a sugar tit," Dan scoffed.

"Jimmy, you know the army can barely protect itself right now," Fargo reminded him. "There's some kind of government in this city, right?"

Jimmy shrugged. "We've got a town council, but government runs only lip deep around here. Most men don't even come to the meetings."

"Happens Injins *do* tie into this town," Dan said, "it could get powerful ugly. Me and Skye has fought Paiutes and Bannocks. They ain't no mission-school Injins—they's stone-cold killers and neither tribe has got a word for 'prisoner of war.'"

"But it's rare for them to attack towns," Jimmy said with stubborn insistence that Fargo believed was desperate hope.

"You heard what Romeo here just said about night attacks. And bear in mind, colt—the redskin victory at Pyramid Lake has put starch in their warbonnets. 'Sides, this puke hole is ripe for a good ass whipping. Half the men in Virginia City talk the he-bear talk, but most ain't never fought redskins. When it's time to burn powder agin savages, their knees will play them false."

"I just recalled something," Fargo said. "There's talk of a heap-big Paiute medicine man named Sis-ki-dee. The army claims he's stirring up the tribes against the white man. A Bannock scout at the fort told me this Sis-ki-dee has the evil road—meaning he dabbles in black magic. If a shaman makes them believe he can turn enemy bullets into sand, Indian warriors will attack anybody."

Jimmy suddenly grinned. "Never mind. I think you're being called to duty, Mr. Fargo."

Jimmy nodded toward the landing on the second floor. Smooth Bore and Tit Bit had found saloon girls to replace them at the gaming tables. Now both women were smiling expectantly at Fargo.

"Wait here, gents," Fargo told his companions. "I'm not one for small talk and neither are they."

"Two at wunst," Snake River Dan said as Fargo stood up and grabbed his Henry. "You got a mile-high opinion of yourself, son. And them two she-bitches don't like being disappointed. See you in the next life, pard."

5

Fargo had watched the sisters slip into the doorway on the left side of the landing. He walked in without knocking and froze midstep at the sight before him. Somehow Smooth Bore and Tit Bit had stripped naked in mere moments and now lay side by side in the big brass bed. Both women had skin like honey poured in sunlight and both were eagerly cosseting their love nests in anticipation of Fargo's skillful ministrations.

"Strip buck," Smooth Bore ordered him. "You *know* what we want to see."

Fargo looked at two of the finest tarts he had ever devoured. Smooth Bore, with her copper red ringlets and a pair of the most impressive loaves Fargo had ever encountered; Tit Bit, with pillow-fanned dark hair, baby-blanket blue eyes, and the shaggy dark mons bush that excited Fargo with its promise of primitive lust and unbridled appetite.

"Ladies . . . this is a true embarrassment of riches."

He shot the bar latch home and propped his rifle against a wall, dropping his shell belt. By now all the female pulchritude had Fargo aroused, a fact that didn't escape Smooth Bore's notice.

"Oh, look, Bit—there's a big snake in those trousers, and I think it's angry."

"Strip buck," Smooth Bore repeated, more breathless this time. "Don't just open your fly like you usually do. We want the whole solid slab of manflesh."

Fargo complied somewhat awkwardly, for he always felt vulnerable to enemy attacks when naked—and especially when barefoot. But these two randy firebrands had him champing at the bit, and he fumbled out of his boots and buckskins. As he stripped he asked them, "So how do we play this hand? How 'bout one girl at a time while the other watches?"

"Oh, poof!" Smooth Bore countered. "A man always finishes quick the first time. That means the second girl will get it longer. No, we're doing it just like us three done in San Francisco, only this time *I* get to sit on your peeder while Bit straddles your face."

"I'll watch you two screw for a while," Tit Bit decided. "That'll get me all het up for a nice ride—God, *look* at that tree limb, Sis."

Fargo kicked out of his trousers, his aroused staff jumping with each heartbeat. Fargo had been in the wilds for weeks, and seeing these two beauties naked was like finding a banquet. He squeezed in between them and shuddered with tingling pleasure when Tit Bit licked his shaft.

"Gosh *dang* you're hard," she marveled. "A buffalo would be proud of that boner. He's gonna explode, Smooth Bore. You best hold on when this stallion gets to bucking."

Smooth Bore sat up, straddled Fargo, and guided his length into her, shuddering and crying out. Fargo was soon bucking like an angry mustang, driving into her over and over and forcing her to orgasmic cries and moans. Unable to sit back long, Tit Bit swung one shapely leg over Fargo's face and lowered the warm rubyfruit lips of her sex onto his mouth. He found her lust-swollen pearl already protruding from its hood of chamois-soft skin and flicked it rapidly with the end of his tongue.

"Skye, you merciless *bastard*!" she screamed after a minute or so of this, a climax suddenly welling inside her. "Oh, you damn bull, that's so nice!"

Tit Bit climaxed so violently that she fell off the bed, and Fargo was glad of it because now it was him and Smooth Bore on a runaway train with an overheated boiler. Her tight little valentine had vise-grip muscles that milked him hard, insistently, sending jolts of pleasure pulsing through him.

Smooth Bore began hard, fast plunges on his man gland and peaked so hard that her sister, eagerly watching, had to catch her—especially when Fargo, his duty to the girls done, took his own heaving pleasure in several powerful, conclusive thrusts. His release was so energetic that he broke a bed board and the mattress caved under them.

Tit Bit sighed. "You know Skye is back when the bed comes down."

Smooth Bore, still lying on the concaved mattress, wrapped a hand around Fargo's semitumescent staff. "Lord, it ought to be its own county."

"Careful," he warned her. "It's a little tender right after."

"It *ought* to be. How many women has this stout yeoman pleased?"

Fargo finally mustered enough strength to squirm out of the cave-in and start pulling on his clothes. "Ladies, it was a pure-dee pleasure."

"Care to go again?" Tit Bit asked. "My turn to ride the rail."

Fargo grinned. "For *you* two I'm not up to fettle."

"Come see us when you are."

When Fargo returned to his friends, a troupe of jugglers, acrobats, and magicians was performing on the stage along the back wall.

"You can still walk?" Snake River Dan greeted him. "After them two worked you over, I figgered we'd have to gather you up with a rake."

"They're little firecrackers," Fargo allowed. "Say, that lady juggler is good."

"Yeah, Nash Booth likes her, too," Jimmy said drily. "You'll notice all three of his 'associates' are with him now. They never miss this show."

"Let's just walk over and kill the sons a bitches right damn now," Dan said on an impulse. "C'mon! Hell, they tried to snuff Fargo's wick—turnabout is fair play. Four Kentucky pills to the melon and it's all over."

"Dan, you got to remember I'm a U.S. deputy marshal," Jimmy protested. "You're inciting to murder."

"All right, stay here and sip your beer, badge-toter. Me and the hungry pecker will do it. Ready, Fargo?"

"Put a stopper on your gob," Fargo snapped. "I prefer legal killing. Right now I'm in bad odor with both Ephraim Cole and Septimus Dunwiddie—and that's just the way I like it. It means we *will* be hugging with Booth and his fellow cockroaches. No need to go blasting away in a saloon and kill innocent customers."

"That's medicine," Dan agreed. "Them entertainers don't deserve to get shot. I've gone kill-crazy in my old age."

"But you were right," Fargo added. "The best way to handle

49

this deal is to strike back quick and hard. I still require more proof before I shoot to kill, but we can at least send in our card."

"Now you're whistling," Dan approved. "Send in the card then send in the lead."

"Don't forget," Jimmy said, "we're still under Territorial governance here, not martial law. We can't break the law—not the big ones, anyhow."

Fargo waved this concern aside. "Nothing like that. Nash and his bunch like giving out nasty surprises, so we'll take a spoke from their wheel. You can sit this one out, Marshal—me and Dan can wangle this one later today."

The old trapper loosed a string of curses. "Fargo, you are the most world-beatingest man I ever knew. You was upstairs just now and got you some pussy—*two* women, mind you—and do your pards get a little? Nary a lick. But comes time to die a dog's death, you're ready to go equal shares with us."

"I ain't got you killed yet, have I? Pipe down. That tongue of yours has been salted in a pickling jar."

Fargo watched Jimmy absently pull a bit of rope from his shirt pocket and work it in his fingers—a habit he repeated often. "What's the rope for?" Fargo asked.

Jimmy shrugged. "This was cut off a rope that was used to hang a man. A sheriff near Stockton told me it's good luck."

"Well," Fargo said, "wake me up when the good luck commences."

Fargo studied Jimmy closer. The young man looked crestfallen and preoccupied. Something was weighing on him and he was keeping it to himself.

"Death threats, right?" Fargo said.

Jimmy's freckled, sunburned face looked startled. "Yeah. Found a note pinned to the jailhouse door. Told me to clear out now or I'll be gunned down."

Fargo surprised him by grinning. "Good. That means the medicine's taking hold. Far as the note—you're in no more danger just because a threat is written down."

The threat that entered the saloon just then, however, was not written down—it walked into the Wicked Sisters with burning black eyes and a hell-and-damnation ferocity that silenced the place. The magician onstage retreated so quickly that he tripped over his own cape and crashed onto a table, collapsing it.

"Slade's bringing the house down," Fargo muttered.

Terrible Jack Slade, clearly drunk, searched the saloon, spotted Fargo, and crossed unsteadily toward his table.

"Plug the bastard, Fargo," Dan muttered. "He plans to jerk it back on you."

"Go to your playhouse, prissy," Fargo replied. "Just stay frosty."

Slade hauled up about two feet from the table. "How are you, Fargo?"

Fargo averted his gaze from Slade's hideous necklace of shriveled, blackened human ears. "Oh, keeping up the strut, Jack, keeping up the strut."

"I saw those vile twats who own this cesspool crawling all over you yesterday. Harken and heed, Trailsman: a woman has seven openings in her body, and the devil can enter any of them."

"Long as he waits his turn," Fargo quipped. "Say, what's all this stirring-and-to-do about midnight next Wednesday?"

Slade's handsome face suddenly looked coy, and he lowered his voice confidentially. "Life is a disease, Fargo, and the only cure is death."

Slade tipped his bowler hat and headed back into the billiards room. Snake River Dan tapped his temple with an index finger. "Room for rent, if you take my drift. He's just babbling crazy talk."

Jimmy shook his head. "I ain't so sure. This talk now ain't his usual line. I think he's got something planned."

"He's insane but dangerous," Fargo agreed. "Maybe even more dangerous than those four hired killers over there measuring us for a coffin."

After describing where Fargo would find the place where Nash Booth and his three minions stayed, Jimmy left the Wicked Sisters to make his rounds. Fargo and Snake River Dan found a place called the Bluebush Café on Center Street serving eggs—at the ungodly price of fifty cents apiece—and stoked their bellies with a piping-hot meal.

"You know," Fargo said as they hoofed it toward the livery, "most people out here don't change their behavior until there's a disaster. It's smarter to head off the disaster, and Jimmy sees

51

that. He's right as rain about the bad sanitation killing more people than bullets do."

"He's a right decent sort," Dan agreed. "It's rare to meet an honest man. Still a mite green, is all. And around here, that could soon make him deader than a can of corned beef. Don't help none that you come down like thunder on Dunwiddie and galled Cole."

"Just stirring up the mix before straining."

They swung into the livery yard, Fargo's vigilant eyes missing nothing. Dan removed his slouch hat and swiped the stringy, greasy hair from his eyes. "C'mon, Fargo, give. What's your plan?"

Fargo grabbed his high-cantled saddle from a rack and lugged it to the Ovaro's stall. "Tell you the straight, old roadster, I don't exactly have one yet. We'll have to reconnoiter first. Maybe do some horseback thinking."

"Ain't like you, Fargo, to make battle plans on the fly."

Fargo cinched the girth and checked his latigos. "Sometimes there's no other choice. Right now we're like a snake trying to get started on loose sand. We can't just deal summary justice without proof or Jimmy takes it in the tail—he hired me, don't forget, and has to answer for my actions. So we'll provoke the local roaches until they react and it's legal to kill them."

Fargo glanced across to the stall occupied by Dan's dish-faced skewbald, jaw dropping in astonishment at what he saw. "Old man, are you giving that animal whiskey?"

"Mescal, to chew it fine. Just a few sips from my hat. This worthless Indian scrub is wild for it. We both do better work with a bracer."

"No wonder that broom tail has a crooked gait. But wait until he can't get the hootch—a horse with the jimjams ain't a pretty sight."

The two men led their mounts into the yard and forked leather, heading west on Center Street. It was late afternoon, a westering sun balanced like a bloodred coin on the Sierra Nevada, and the street and plank-board walks filled and thickened with carousers.

Jimmy had explained that Booth and his gang lived in a mine building behind the Schofield, once used as a powder magazine—and the probable reason, Fargo concluded, why they commandeered it for themselves.

"How do you know these hard cases will even be there?" Dan asked.

"I don't—I got no crystal ball and I don't live in their pockets. But they're night riders, remember? Night's coming on, and Jimmy told me those four take no meals in town. If you were a hardworking, murdering scum of a night rider, wouldn't you get outside of some grub before riding out?"

The two horsebackers cleared town and trotted their mounts down the winding slope. Dan made a last check of his powder loads while Fargo flicked the riding thong off the hammer of his Colt.

As the tinny clamor of Virginia City faded behind them, Fargo heard the hissing, clanging racket of the mines below growing louder. But it was silent in the grainy twilight of the road except for the dull clopping of their horses' hooves and the light clinking of bit rings. It was the kind of eerie silence Fargo knew from previous encounters—a silence that grew more and more unnatural until it exploded in a kill cry.

The tree cover on their right turned into a wide swath of timber-denuded land, wood used to brace the stopes of several hard-rock mines. Looking at the vast, ugly sprawl of the Schofield mining site, much of which resembled bomb rubble, Fargo felt a strong stirring of nostalgia for the pristine West he had once trailed through, a place blissfully free of eastern capital and ruin. Strong will, optimism, and blind ignorance—all causing a foolish underestimation of the dangers and damage to the land and the tribes.

"Goldang ugly, ain't it?" Dan asked, as if reading Fargo's thoughts. "And them hydraulic operations is washing away half of the Sierra range. Big mountains turned into hummocks."

"It comes straight from hell, all right," Fargo said. "Still, it also involves pluck and grit, and I have to admire that much."

The two men stayed behind long piles of ore tailings and circled around the mine. A large meadow of timothy and clover, deliberately spared to provide graze for dray animals, separated the old powder magazine from the Schofield's big headframe.

Fargo and Dan reined in, keeping a windbreak of juniper trees between them and the building.

"Mebbe you was right, Trailsman," Dan said. "I count four horses in that rope corral. Sore-used, too."

53

"Doesn't mean the scum buckets are here," Fargo reminded him. "Hell, that place is a strong box."

He noted the thick double-planked walls, loopholes later added for rifles, with narrow air vents instead of windows. "A good blockade in a shooting scrape."

But Fargo saw other, more favorable details. The only door was hinged to swing outward, and old barrels stacked on one side of the square building made it easy to climb onto the roof. Most important, the men had added a stovepipe chimney for a cooking stove, and puffs of smoke drifted from it now.

"We'll tether the horses here," Fargo said. "I hate to do it, but we better muzzle 'em with our belts. Those louts can't hear anything in the house, but if one comes outside he could hear a whinny."

When they were set to cross the clearing, Fargo explained his plan to Snake River Dan, who grinned his approval. Fargo left his Henry in its scabbard, freeing his hands to climb. They bent low at the waist and sped toward the partial cover of the corral. But Fargo's plan suddenly suffered a wrench when the door swung open and Chilly Davis emerged into the fading sunlight.

"Eat dirt," Fargo hissed, and both men dropped like stones.

Fargo cursed the luck. Grass was sparse in this meadow and barely high enough to cover a shoe. But Davis didn't glance toward them. He ducked into the corral, and Fargo saw he carried a horseshoe and a shoeing hammer.

"Steady, old man," Fargo told Dan. "This won't be long."

Davis led a nervous but docile gelding, a dark cream with black mane and tail, into better light and began pulling the rear offside shoe.

Dan, one eye asquint, got a closer look at the horses. His face wrinkled in disgust. "I never seen anything to equal it. A man can't call himself a Westerner and treat horseflesh like that. Great balls of fire look at Booth's ginger."

Fargo picked his teeth with a weed as he studied the flat-withered horse. The flanks were galled by girth sores and gaping saddle sores, and ugly lumps of scar tissue showed where the gelding had been spurred deep in the shoulders.

Both men lay flat waiting for Davis to finish his task. Dan annoyed Fargo by sucking on a piece of sassafras candy close to Fargo's ear. Dan was nearly toothless and made liquid slapping noises that sounded disgusting to Fargo. Just as he opened his mouth to complain, Davis headed back into the dwelling.

"All right," Fargo said, "you know your part. Work fast. If they spot us and stay inside, no point in us making a stand—they're well forted up. Just light a shuck for your horse."

Fargo burst toward the stack of barrels while Dan headed for a pile of kindling beside the door. In less than a minute the old frontiersman had wedged the door shut tight with wood chips. Fargo, meantime, had gained the roof and was cat-footing toward the chimney.

"Listen, Booth," Sam Watson said, "we got that nancy boy Cole banging our ears about how we gotta be more 'tactful,' and we got Dunwiddie telling us we're hauling back on the reins too much. Let *them* lily-white silk cravats haul the hard freight just once."

"Brother, you ain't just birding," chimed in Willard Jones. He and Watson sat at a crude deal table dipping soda biscuits into the pot liquor from a beef stew. "Cole acting all biggity like his shit don't stink. Them perfumed poncy men are pulling in a bonanza, and all we get is the hind tit."

Nash Booth sat on a nearby nail keg rolling a quirly. The scornful twist of his mouth made him look predatory and ruthless. "Both you little bitches need to reach inside your britches and see if you're men. Christ, all you do is whine."

Both men clamped their teeth rather than retort. With Booth a man never knew.

"Don't queer the deal," Booth said, his dead-button eyes unnerving. "Let Cole and Dunwiddie parade their fancy duds and play the big bugs. When the time is right, we'll settle accounts with both of them. For now, though, it's Fargo we got to worry about."

Chilly Davis, nursing a bottle of potent mash, snorted. "*If* you believe newspaper hokum."

"Horseshit, lame brain. Fargo hangs on like a tick until his enemies are destroyed. He can track better than a Messy Apache, shoot better than a Texas Ranger, and he can sink that Arkansas toothpick into a man's heart at thirty paces. If we fail to plant him, I'll guarantee it—our cake is dough."

"Damn, Nash," Jones said, "I ain't never heard you talk up any man like you just done."

"Boys, if I'm joking I'm choking. Fargo is a mighty potent force. Either we put the quietus on him, and quick, or for us it's the knot for sure."

Booth, too, felt a hair-trigger contempt for both Cole and Dunwiddie, but they were money in his pocket and that was all that mattered—for the moment. Fargo, however, was a different pair of shoes altogether. Booth licked his quirly, twisted the ends, and struck a match on his rough rawhide vest, leaning into the flame. His dead gaze settled on Watson and Davis.

"And *you* two stumblebums . . . letting Fargo queer our grab on the Gramlich claim. Valiant as Essex lions, you are."

Watson, juice dribbling down his chin, scowled. "Ease off, why'n'cha? You just got done sounding off on how dangerous this crusader is. Now you're pissing and moaning on account Fargo bollixed up the Gramlich deal for us. You can't have it both ways."

Booth suddenly glanced overhead. "You boys hear anything just now from topside?"

"Settle down," Jones said. "Christ, Fargo is giving you the fantods."

"It's this goddamn oven heat," Booth snapped. "Do you have to cook at the hottest part of the day? We're on the edge of a desert and this place is a closed box."

Booth scowled at the simple beehive stove the others had rigged up. "You don't need them hot embers now. Smother 'em with dirt."

You don't need them hot embers now. Smother 'em with dirt.

Fargo had already dropped a dozen cartridges, one by one, down the stovepipe chimney when he heard Booth's order.

Irritation swept over Fargo. He chastised himself: Just a few minutes earlier and the show would have gone on.

"Ahh, I ain't even eaten," Fargo heard one of Booth's underlings complain. "'Sides, I done it last time. It's Sam's turn."

"Your ass, Willard! It's Chilly's turn to tamp the fire."

Fargo grinned in the gathering twilight. Criminal laziness might save the show yet.

"Shit, piss, and corruption!" Booth roared like an incensed bull. "One of you cockchafers had best snuff them embers or I'll snuff—"

A bullet detonated below, shocking Booth into silence. A second, a third round cracked off, slugs tearing into various parts of the building. By the time the fourth shot cooked off, full-blown panic gripped the men below. More rounds erupting all around them, somebody rushed the door and then cursed when it refused to budge. Fargo crept to the edge of the roof overlooking the door, waiting with his Colt to hand and his spare cylinder tucked behind his belt.

"Open the son of a bitch!" Nash Booth roared. "Open it, I said! We're rag tatters if we stay in here!"

Fargo glanced toward the corral and frowned. Snake River Dan was supposed to be hunkered down behind the corral out of sight. But he had crept up to the front corner, partially exposed, and too late Fargo realized why.

He whistled sharply to get the old salt's attention, signaling him to draw back. But Dan gave him a defiant grin and waved both Dragoon pistols.

It was too late anyway—the front door split open with a thumping, splintering sound, and burly Chilly Davis shot out into the yard, losing his footing. With the last rounds still cracking like whips inside the dwelling, the other three burst out, trampling Davis in their haste. The men sprinted toward the nearby Schofield, blindly wing-shooting with their revolvers as they ran.

Fargo had planned to set up a hot but nonlethal crossfire with Dan, but the old man had blood in his eye for Willard Jones. He was easy to spot in his yellow-corded cavalry hat. His face glowing with the revenge need, Dan suddenly leaped out into full view.

"From now to eternity, you rat bastard, it's hot pitchforks for you!"

But Dan's dramatic showdown turned into a farce when he fired both Colts and produced only the puny popping sound of the detonator caps—the powder loads had clumped.

Jones pivoted deftly and shucked out a barking iron, opening up on the old trapper at close range. Cursing, Fargo popped a round into Jones' arm to send him running. But by now the others had spotted Fargo on the roof, and whistling lead thickened the air around him.

Thanks to Dan's stupidity an easy raid had turned into a root-hog-or-die situation. Never one to get bogged down in an uneven shootout, Fargo opted to gamble rather than simply take what was dished out. He sat back on his legs and fanned the hammer, pausing only to insert the spare cylinder.

Fargo blew off two hats and the rest of his bullets chunked into the dirt at the gang's feet. As he had hoped, the furious lead bath sent them racing to the mine. But not before Booth shouted, "You'll get it in the neck, Fargo!"

"Now we're up against it, Methuselah," Fargo said in a grim tone as he climbed down, face powder-blackened. "You just *had* to brace Jones, didn't you?"

"*Plague* take that son of a bitch! And you, too, Fargo! Hell, I nearbout had him killed till you stuck your oar in my boat."

"You cantankerous idiot, he was about to air you out. I saved your worthless hide."

"Mebbe so, but christsakes, *why* did you just wing the scavenger? You coulda tunneled through his brainpan at that range."

"Much like a gelded horse, you just don't get it, do you? This ain't the time for killing shots."

Dan turned solemnly emphatic. "The very sight of that jasper makes my blood go sour. I told you what he done to me. Would you let some criminal son of a bitch kill the Ovaro and get away with it?"

"Never mind Jones," Fargo ordered in a tone he seldom used with friends. "Or did you throw in with me and Jimmy just so you could kill Jones?"

"What's it signify? I'm here, ain't I?"

"For how long? Until Jones cops it?"

By now the two men had reached their horses. The Ovaro, long used to shooting scrapes, calmly greeted Fargo by nuzzling his shoulder. Fargo slid the Henry into its scabbard and knelt to untie the hobbles.

"All right, Dan," he said quietly in the gathering darkness. "This is no time for mavericks. The odds are stacked against us in this town, and I got a bad feeling on this one. If you deliberately ruin our plans once again, I swear I'll kill you for cause."

6

Dawn came and went with amazing speed in the white sand desert, where the medicine man Sis-ki-dee and his Paiute Sash Warriors had made their latest camp. The shaman sat now in the entrance to his wickiup listening to a few old women sing "Song to the New Sun Rising." The battle chief known as Plenty Coups sat close by stringing a new bow.

"From where we sit now to where the sun walks the sky— this is how far the hair-face invaders say their white-eye law rules. We were fools to ever let them cross our tribal lands for mere tribute. *All* should have been killed—not even their unborn are innocent."

Sis-ki-dee paused, his fierce, burning eyes gazing out across the desolate wastes. This dry and sterile land, southeast of the white man's lodge circle called Virginia City, was almost barren of growth, game, and even carrion birds. But bleached bones were easy enough to find.

"You have eyes to see," Sis-ki-dee continued. "This is a hard place no man could covet. Only by constant raiding can we feed ourselves and our pony herd. Only two sleeps ago we were forced to kill ten of our ponies for meat. The other tribes refuse to stay any longer."

"Only us," Plenty Coups said bitterly. "Even our battle cousins, the Shoshones and the Bannocks, only return to join us in war. We Paiutes chose to remain and master this land no one else wants."

"These are words I can pick up and examine," Sis-ki-dee agreed. "And then the hair-faces found the glittering yellow rocks here. If we let them take our land, they will multiply in numbers too great to count. The red man is in peril of his very existence."

Plenty Coups nodded, his sun-leathered face expressionless.

Copper and silver brassards protected his upper arms. The eagle-and-bone whistle thrust into his topknot was used for signaling his elite braves in an attack.

"I have ears for all this," he said. "They swarm over us like maggots in a carcass. But they have the thunder sticks that kill from far off."

"There are ways to kill," Sis-ki-dee assured him, "besides closing with the enemy."

Plenty Coups pointed to his nearby war pony. The oak war club lashed to it bristled with deadly spikes. "These ways you speak of are for cowardly Poncas. A warrior kills in fair combat. I will die with my face toward the enemy."

Sis-ki-dee's panther-scarred face hardened with contempt. "You boast too much of dying. Better to live and slay your enemy. Add your noble 'honor' to an arrow and you will have an arrow."

This was outright blasphemy to a Paiute warrior, but Plenty Coups feared Sis-ki-dee's skill at evil medicine—and his complete control over this band. Sis-ki-dee was branded the Contrary Warrior after rebelling against the tribal council, which argued for peace with the white skin invaders. He had spent most of his time in the Green River area after his tribe banished him, and it didn't take him long to divide the tribe after he returned.

Even now Plenty Coups felt a stirring of rebellion as he stared at Sis-ki-dee's buckskin leggings—a gruesome sight even to a hardened warrior. They were decorated with entire fingernails pulled from white victims including the tiny ones of children and infants. This Sis-ki-dee lived by the night, roaming far into the mysterious darkness when other braves huddled in their lodges. During his birth, it was widely said, a wild pony galloped by the lodge, marking him as one who would follow the evil road through life.

"You have talked my men into following you," Plenty Coups said. "But you know how the Sash Warriors fight. Why ask us to kill like unclean white men?"

"Yes, I know your warrior 'code.' The Sash Warrior shows his resolve by pinning his sash to the ground and fighting to the death on that spot. These are the same fools who think feather prayer sticks can turn enemy bullets into sand. No wonder the red man is being slaughtered like the buffalo. Hate me if you will, I am indifferent. But you *know* I am right because you are a warrior. Our time is now or soon it will be never."

Reluctantly Plenty Coups nodded affirmation. For a time the tribes of this area had been content to let these foolish and curious beings pass through their nations for the price of some coffee or sugar, perhaps a cow. But the great pale skin migration had tapered off toward the end of the time the white man's wintercount called the eighteen-fifties, in part because warpath Indians were no longer amused by these possessive intruders and began to make their lives hazardous.

"You still say we must attack them in their lodges?" Plenty Coups asked. "You know it is not our custom to attack a fortedup enemy."

"Spoken straight arrow, and it is those very customs the white man counts on to feel safe. They *know* we do not fight in their fashion, and that is why we should."

Sis-ki-dee pushed to his feet. "Speaking of these matters . . . come with me. You have not seen what Young Man and his clan brought back from their raid besides three bloody scalps on their sashes."

Sis-ki-dee headed toward a trio of bent-branch wickiups used as common storage for plunder. A young squaw in a doeskin dress adorned with dyed quills saw Sis-ki-dee coming toward her and scurried away. His hold over this band, he knew, was based on fear, not respect—a thought that coaxed his lips into a brief smile.

Behind the three wickiups was a sturdier lodge made of poles and hides sewn together. Sis-ki-dee flipped the entrance flap aside. Bright early-morning sunlight poured into the lodge, revealing six stout wooden kegs. Plenty Coups shot him a quizzical glance.

"White man's gunpowder," Sis-ki-dee explained. "It makes the big-thundering explosions and sets many fires. These were meant for blowing up the ground to expose the yellow rocks."

"We know nothing of this thundering powder," Plenty Coups objected. "We do not even have the long sticks that spit smoke and kill."

"*I* know of it," Sis-ki-dee said. "I learned about it in the

Green River country. We could steal into their lodge circle at night—"

Here Plenty Coups visibly paled. "Have you grazed loco weed? The ancient laws of the Manitous forbid *any* red warrior from leaving the camp circle at night."

"Add your Manitous to spider leavings," Sis-ki-dee retorted, "and you will have spider leavings. There is no god but the boldest killer."

Plenty Coups was courageous but not the brightest spark in the fire, and Sis-ki-dee's reference to pitiless killing of whites appealed to him.

"Only look to the south of us," Sis-ki-dee reminded him. "Only three tribes—the Comanches, the Kiowas, and the Apaches—are successful in exterminating whites. And all three fight in cover of darkness."

"But we already know," Plenty Coups objected, "that the white-eyes keep sentries out at night. The open desert around their lodges is white and reflects moonlight. How could we ever draw close enough to place the thunder powder?"

As if timed to answer Plenty Coups' question, a sudden, furious snarling of angry dogs reached them from the far side of camp.

"We could not approach them safely," Sis-ki-dee said, "without a diversion. One that will keep the paleface devils from noticing us until it is too late. And this place hears me when I say we *will* send these evil intruders back to the white devil who spawned them."

Fargo's third day in Virginia City dawned hot and stagnant as most did in the summertime deserts. He washed in the buckets provided out back of the flophouse, ever vigilant for foolish men.

"Take it by and large," Snake River Dan said as the two men rolled their blankets, "we're lucky to be alive. We got Cole, Dunwiddie, and Booth all on the scrap agin us."

"That's trouble and more," Fargo agreed. "But we expect it. I'm starting to fear we're about to be blindsided."

"What's your drift?"

"Indians," Fargo said bluntly. "Most likely Paiutes. I think the uprising at Pyramid Lake has emboldened them. The signs point to an attack. I told Jimmy to worry about the mess in town

62

first, but I'm having second thoughts. We might have a two-front battle."

"Good," Dan spat out. "Ain't that what you want? You been beatin' your gums about how you're gonna make the killers come to you. More the merrier, anh?"

"You *had* a few teeth left, old man, when you woke up."

The two friends met Jimmy at the Bluebush Café for biscuits and scrapple.

"I got another death threat," he said as he joined them. "Some yahoo wrapped it around a rock and tossed it through the jailhouse window."

"I don't set much store by death threats," Fargo said. "If a man's set in his mind on killing you, what does he gain with a warning?"

"Death threats," Dan echoed. "It's coals to Newcastle. This whole goddamn shebang is a death threat."

Fargo watched Jimmy sit with his broad shoulders hunched as if to ward off wind. He plucked the piece of rope from his pocket and idly started working it.

"I was you," Fargo advised, "I'd chuck that hangman's rope."

"It's spozed to be good luck."

"Yeah? It wasn't too damn much good luck for the man it hanged, was it?"

But Fargo felt sorry for the kid and pumped some optimism into his tone. "Look here, boys. No need to be walking on your lower lips. I'd say we're making some headway."

"In a pig's patootie," Dan retorted.

"We are," Fargo insisted. "Or at least some of the breaks are going our way. It looks like Ephraim Cole, a soft-handed board-walker with piss-poor judgment of men, has come to regret putting Nash Booth and his fellow vultures on the payroll. For us, that's an enemy divided."

"The man *said* he regrets it?" Dan demanded. "His own mouth-word?"

"Even better, he wants to hire me to kill Booth before Booth kills him."

"Holy Hannah," Jimmy said, laying his fork down. "Sounds like half the town's going to kill the other half."

"That Cole is rolling in it," Dan said. "You kill Booth for him, you won't need these shit jobs you take for the army."

"Yeah, knucklehead, I should hire out as a common murderer. Booth and his killers make my skin crawl, but if I kill Booth, it'll be an even draw."

"And right after, you'll walk on water, uh?"

"Well," Jimmy pitched in, "Skye's right—we did win a small skirmish. Bo Gramlich has wised up. Since you saved his claim, he drinks only beer. More important, he's formed a partnership with several other prospectors. They cover each other night and day. Other prospectors are doing the same thing."

"Good," Fargo said emphatically. "I wouldn't call that small potatoes. They need to stand up as an armed group."

"By the way," Jimmy added, "Bo said if we need shooters, him and some friends are ready to help. Bo's a good man when he ain't three sheets to the wind."

"You think any of those fellows could get me a stick or two of dynamite?" Fargo asked.

Jimmy looked startled. "Why?"

Fargo lifted one shoulder. "Why not? It can be damn useful."

"I'll see about it. Mostly the mines have it, but some of the prospectors use it to move rocks and such."

Fargo watched Dan, whose seat was behind Jimmy's, quickly pull the rattlesnake skin from his possibles bag and flash it. He put it right back, but Fargo knew that Jimmy was in for an unpleasant shock. The three men emerged into the bright heat, their heads on a swivel for trouble.

"I think we need to split up and patrol the town," Fargo said. "Nobody plays the hero, right? For now just look and listen. But first let's hoof it down to the saloon for a draught. We're mighty popular there, evidently, and we don't want to high-hat our friends."

"It's a dirty shame," Jimmy piped up. "With the killers and claim jumpers under control, this could be a bang-up sort of a town. There's plenty of money for civic works like ditches and sewers. 'Course, it would still need more than just a few Easter and Christmas Christians."

"Well, when you get all the Christians," Snake River Dan said as he burst into a wide grin, "you better put the kibosh on *that*."

He didn't need to point. Straight ahead, raising a yellow-brown cloud of dust on Center Street, came an onrushing wall of naked female flesh: the running of the whores. Men cheered them along the way with shouts and gunshots.

"You know," Dan opined as the women began to pass them, "a woman's tits look silly when she's running full tilt."

"Hey, Buckskins!" shouted the blonde who had greeted him yesterday. "A free ride for you! Ask for Jenny at the Wicked Sisters!"

"*Free.*" Dan chuckled. "What else? They'll get ice water in hell before Skye Fargo pays for tail."

"Yeah, but she's the pretty sporting gal in town," Jimmy said. "She goes at the top rate."

Another two blocks remained until they reached the Wicked Sisters, and Fargo kept his hand near his holster. The street was crowded, and there were plenty of alleys and windows to worry about.

"Skye, were you a mountain man like Dan?" Jimmy asked.

Fargo shook his head. "You best study up on your history. The beaver trapped out and most of the mountain men had all hung up their axes by the time I was shaving. But I met some including Peg-leg Smith. Amputated his own leg then whittled a stump to replace it. I learned my lore from those old grizzlies."

"Them was the shining times," Dan said solemnly. "The true mountain man fled from any place that started peopling up."

True, Fargo thought, but in their headlong flight they also created the very paths and trails civilization used to overtake them and create powder kegs like Virginia City.

Jimmy suddenly froze in place, staring straight ahead down the street. "God's galoshes!"

Fargo and Dan followed Jimmy's gaze and could not credit their eyes. "Ain't *this* a pretty kettle of fish?" Dan said, grinning wickedly.

Terrible Jack Slade, dressed in a black frock coat left open to show off his magnificent concho belt, rode into town astride a trotting dapple gray. His handsome face was serene despite the rope tied to his saddle horn and the corpse it had drag-hanged— a common practice where trees and law were scarce.

"Jack," Marshal Helzer greeted him, "you know lynchings ain't legal since this town agreed to federal law."

Slade reined in. "Oh, glory be, Marshal, it was nothing like that. This dung beetle here claimed I knew his wife in the Old

65

Testament sense. He tried to shoot me from ambush, so I beat him to death in self-defense. I merely tied the rope to his neck so I could drag the body closer for the pigs to eat it."

Jimmy had already knelt to examine the body. "I don't know, Jack," he spoke up nervously. "There's no marks on the body except from your rope. You said you beat him to death."

Slade smiled. His indifferent confidence put Fargo on edge.

"Any witnesses?" Jimmy added.

"Not a one," Jack said from a straight face. "You know how it is."

It was all a crock and everybody there knew it, but Slade's stories were always impossible to disprove.

"Ahuh. I hear bruised meat makes for tougher eating," Snake River Dan quipped from a face blank as a slate.

"So does *older* meat," Slade retorted, and Dan took a sudden interest in his own moccasins.

Slade aimed a warning gaze at Jimmy. His manner combined mockery with genuine outrage. "Marshal, every time there's trouble around here, the whoreson shirkers howl for my hide. You see, a man of strong opinions is never forgiven, and I have strong opinions."

Fargo laughed. "Jack, it's not your *opinions* that get folks all riled up. It just seems that a lot of people"—Fargo glanced at the corpse with its bloated black face—"are took dead around you."

"Decent people?" Jack demanded before gigging the dapple gray forward.

"Holy Christ, Jimmy," Fargo said. "Stay on him like heat rash. But don't close-herd him. I hope he's just playing the larks with us about trouble next Wednesday. But my gut tells me different."

"Say!" Jimmy pulled up short. "That business about tough meat . . . you fellows don't suppose *he* means to eat the body?"

"Reminds me of a good windy," Snake River Dan said. "These two cannibals find a corpse in the jungle, see? 'You start at the head and I'll start at the feet,' one of 'em says, 'and we'll meet in the middle.' They commence to eatin', and after a bit the first cannibal calls out, 'How you doing there?' The second one says, 'I'm having a ball.' 'Slow down!' the first one yells. 'You're eating too fast.' Now, ain't that a ripsnorter?"

Jimmy laughed politely while Fargo pushed open the batwings and led the way into the Wicked Sisters. Business was still light and Fargo instantly recognized the chiseled face with its red-gold scruff of whiskers: Nash Booth sharing his usual table with his minions.

"I see Willard Jones has got a bandaged shoulder," Dan said. "Looks like you winged him good."

The three men had just bellied up to the plank counter when Booth spotted them.

"Boys," Fargo muttered, "if any of those bastards clears leather we're gonna pop 'em over right here and now. You know the rule: drawing a weapon in a saloon shows intent to kill."

"All right," Jimmy said, "but watch out for friendlies."

Whatever Booth had in mind, he dropped the idea when he saw the steely resolve in Fargo's granite-chiseled features. "Hey, Fargo!" he called over. "Changed your mind about working for me yet?"

"I got a rule," Fargo replied.

"Yeah? What's that?"

"I don't draw wages from any man I plan to kill."

Even from the bar Fargo saw a sudden anger squall in Booth's normally dead eyes. "That's mighty tall talk, Fargo."

"Naturally," Fargo replied amiably. "I'm a tall man."

Tim Bowman, fighting off a grin, leaned across the counter. "What's yours, boys?"

"Barley pop for me and the marshal," Fargo said, planking a gold dollar, "and a shot of red-eye for Moses here. But just one—he can chase it with a beer."

"A teamster was in here just now," Tim said. "Says a gunpowder shipment for the Dundee mine was heisted by Paiutes a few days ago."

Fargo's eyebrows almost touched when he frowned. "Paiutes? Last I heard, they don't even have guns yet."

Snake River Dan twisted a finger into his soup-strainer mustache, mulling all this. "Seems a mite queer to me," he said.

"A mite," Fargo agreed. "They might not even know what it was they stole. Or maybe—" He looked at Jimmy. "This crazy-by-thunder medicine man I told you about—Sis-ki-dee—was around white men back in the Yellowstone country. He could've learned about black powder."

"You said he wasn't a war leader," Jimmy pointed out.

"Right. He's a wichasha wakan, a shaman. But shamans can sometimes control the battle chiefs."

Fargo watched Smooth Bore and Tit Bit descend the stairs carrying the cards and markers to set up the monte and faro games. Smooth Bore looked especially pretty and curvaceous in an organdy-trimmed dress. Both women blew kisses toward Fargo.

Fargo watched the customers stare hungrily at the two beautiful saloon keepers.

"A few whores ain't enough," Fargo said. "These boys are woman hungry and that can spell trouble. I saw a fight over a whore in Santa Fe leave twelve men dead."

"So who got the whore?" Dan demanded.

Fargo grinned. "Well, I was the only one still alive. Seemed a damn shame to waste her."

"Red Jonson," Jimmy said, "ran a string of whores above his Purple Door saloon, but so many sporting gals got beat up and cut that I had to send them packing. Smooth Bore and Tit Bit don't have that problem here because they know how to handle men."

Dan snorted. "They oughter. They've *handled* plenty."

"Your brother told me," Fargo said to Jimmy, "that the Miners' Committee voted to provide some entertainment besides saloons. The hell happened?"

"Well, the thing of it is—cockfighting and ratting go over great guns in these boomtowns, and those are both saloon sports. But the grand event is the weekly bull-and-bear fight held in that big pit on the western edge of town."

Fargo grinned. "Yeah, and the fight ain't the big attraction. It's the wagers on the outcome."

"The hell you expect, Fargo?" Dan chimed in. "Lemonade socials and cider parties? You sound like that Loretta Perkins—she means to bring 'culture' to Virginia City, too. She's even stocked a library that's got cobwebs over the door."

"No," Fargo gainsaid, watching Booth and his cronies. "I mean to help Jimmy improve sanitation."

Both men stared at him. "Sanitation?" Dan repeated.

"Sure. We're going to wash the shit out of the streets."

The three men retrieved their horses and, at first, patrolled Virginia City together within the town limits. As a late-morning sun took on heat and weight, Fargo ventured out beyond town into the burning white sand.

"We're standing on dynamite, hoss," Snake River Dan warned when they were a couple of miles east of town. "They's enough red sons out here to fill up hell."

"Nothing ventured, nothing gained. We need to read any sign we can find."

At times the wind gusted with maniacal force, the stinging grit cutting deep. Fargo studied the flat, barren landscape remembering that Paiutes liked to hide in covered holes and rise up to ambush an enemy.

"Dan," Jimmy shouted above the wind, "I b'lieve your horse has pulled up lame."

"Don't credit your eyes, colt. He's just faking to avoid work. Watch."

Sure enough, the skewbald suddenly began "limping" on the opposite leg.

"Lazy bastard," Dan said fondly.

"Damn straight he's got lazy," Fargo said. "Giving a horse mescal will do that. Say, here's medicine," he added, spotting horse droppings.

They were so old that the tracks around them had been blown over. Fargo tugged rein and threw off, kneeling with Jimmy to examine the droppings. He broke some apart and the high grain content told him they were white men's horses. Or possibly Indian ponies fed on stolen grain.

"Soldiers or teamsters," Fargo guessed, heading back toward the Ovaro.

He paused for a few minutes, staring off into the hazy, desolate distance. He saw thousands of square miles of bleached white sand, scraggly sage, black rocks and dead mountains with neither plant nor animal life. Terra damnata, Captain Pete Helzer called it, and Fargo couldn't think of a better name.

A sudden, almost feminine shriek made the hair on Fargo's arms stand up. He shucked out his Colt, expecting a fandango, and instead saw Jimmy running into the desert at a two-twenty clip while Dan rolled on the ground, howling with mirth.

"That lad *is* scairt to death of rattlesnakes," Dan managed between peals of mirth. "Look, Fargo."

The old salt sat up and pointed to Jimmy's right stirrup, where he had artfully wrapped the snake skin to look like a coiled serpent. Fargo, too, burst into laughter—life on the frontier was a jarring mix of sheer terror and mind-numbing boredom, and a good practical joke was heaven sent.

A sheepish Jimmy returned to his horse. Dan imitated his girlish shriek and the kid colored like a bumpkin.

"All right, children," Fargo said. "Let's give it another mile before we head back to your sandbox."

"Let's not and say we did," Dan retorted. "This hoss is fond of his scalp."

"If you lose it you won't have to comb it," Fargo said. "C'mon, let's make tracks."

They had ridden perhaps three-quarters of a mile when Fargo spotted the clue he had hoped not to find—the fresh tracks of unshod ponies.

"Not quite three miles from town," he said. "A small scouting party. It wouldn't mean much by day, but these braves rode out after dark. And to most Indians leaving the camp circle after dark is unheard of—the night belongs to the Windigo, the evil spirit, and to monsters like Rawhead and Bloody Bones."

"How do you know these tracks were made after dark?" Jimmy asked.

"Notice all those big rocks that are turned over? Daylight riders would've missed them."

"That's pesticatin'," Dan agreed. "Onliest tribe I know of that ranges at night is the Comanche. And sometimes the Apache."

"This bunch have one hell of a mission," Fargo agreed. "And since there ain't a damn thing out here, guess who they mean to attack."

After returning to Virginia City the three men split up and patrolled separately. Fargo didn't like what he was seeing. The rank-and-file thugs in canvas trousers were out in a show of well-armed force. And the smug glances they cast his way made it clear to Fargo that *he* was their favorite boy.

The hot, still afternoon gave way to a cool and breezy evening. Fargo headed toward Raisin Street, a later addition to Virginia City that held some of the finer homes in town. It didn't seem a likely trouble spot, but Fargo wanted to know how much of the town the "special deputies" considered their range.

He found the street surprisingly quiet and peaceful. Only artful engineering had allowed such a wide street on a steep mountain slope. A few of the homes were turreted mansions complete with carriage houses. As Fargo rode past a more modest two-story home, he caught a pleasant sight in the corner of one eye. The curtains of an upstairs window were partially drawn, and a nearly naked woman had just moved into his view.

Fargo watched, feeling a stirring of arousal, as she stepped out of her frilly lace pantalets. The exciting contrast between her full breasts and tiny waist made him wonder. Playing a hunch, he pulled the brass binoculars from a saddlebag and took a closer look.

"Well, now," Fargo said aloud, grinning. "Miss Loretta Perkins in the flesh."

All her flesh. Fargo marveled at her ivory smoothness and pointy plum-colored nipples. She moved slightly to reach for a dressing robe, and Fargo torqued his body in the saddle to follow her, marveling at the sculpted perfection of her hips and Georgia-peach ass. In his total absorption he didn't realize he was leaning farther and farther out of the saddle. All of an instant, he plunged downward and landed on a white picket fence, loudly splintering a section of it.

Cursing hotly, uninjured but feeling like a damn fool, Fargo tried to free a trapped leg just as the upstairs window banged open. Although the street was mostly dark, when Loretta plunged her head out of the window she could clearly see a buckskin-clad man sprawled ass-over-applecart, binoculars still in hand.

"My soul alive!"

Fargo acted quickly to forestall her rebuke. "Hello there, Miss Perkins. Something must have spooked my horse."

She couldn't suppress a tight smile of triumph. Those binoculars told the story. "A half truth is a whole lie, Mr. Fargo."

"Yeah? Then a half lie must be the whole truth." Fargo finally freed himself and pushed to his feet.

"Well, it *did* give my heart a jump to hear the fence come crashing down."

"I'll pay for the damage."

"Yes, my father will insist on that. So . . . did you see anything interesting?"

"Oh, quite an eyeful," Fargo conceded.

"Did you like what you saw?"

"Fell off my horse, didn't I? Say, speaking of what I saw—what is a woman like you doing in a heller like this? You belong back in the States where there's balls and lectures and other culture vultures like you."

"That's simple. I am a follower of Diderot, the French genius famous for his encyclopedias. I came here to spread enlightenment—in fact, I started the new library here in town."

Fargo resisted making a crack about cobweb traps. "Enlightenment? Most of these men aren't even town broke, if you take my drift."

"No matter," she insisted. "The mass of men, even here, *can* be decently educated and refined."

Fargo laughed. "Neither gospel nor gunpowder can reform them. Especially not when there's gold and silver to be had."

"Well, you're wrong about that. But you were right about something else."

"That being . . . ?"

"When you said, last time we talked, that I *want* to be on your mind—just like you're on mine. I've been taught to sleep with my hands outside the covers. That hasn't been easy since first seeing you."

"In that case why don't I just slip up into your room?"

"I'd like that," she admitted. "But I don't dally with men who frequent brothels, and there's a rumor you have been with both the owners of the Wicked Sisters—at the same time. Are you guilty of such perversion?"

Fargo wasn't sure what "perversion" meant any more than he had ever heard of Dider-whosis. But he was reprieved from answering her loaded question by a querulous male voice.

"Loretta, who in blue blazes are you talking to up there?"

"Good-bye," she whispered, closing the window.

Fargo vaulted into the saddle and cleared out, knowing fathers could be just as dangerous as husbands. He headed back up the mountain slope toward the raucous chaos of Center Street. As usual, drunks, killers, and bullies thronged the unpaved street, and the hollow pop of gunfire erupted every few minutes.

Fargo trotted the Ovaro past the dark maw of an alley entrance. Abruptly a young girl's terrified voice cried out *"Ayudame!"* in Spanish. "Help me!"

The Trailsman hauled back on the reins and then threw them forward to hold his stallion in place. He dropped down light and quiet and penetrated the inky fathoms of darkness in the alley. About thirty feet in, a huge pile of garbage and debris choked off half the alley.

A match flared to life, briefly revealing the sordid tableau. Fargo saw three canvas-pantsed regulators, wearing the billed caps of the Yellow Jacket mine, stripping a scared young Mexican girl who was begging for mercy in Spanish.

Anger shortened his breath, but only for a few heartbeats. Experience took over and he willed himself calm. The perfect moment, for Fargo, was when he became both participant and observer at the same time—as he was becoming now.

He shucked out his gun and stepped behind the pile. A lantern glowed to life in the building behind them, casting a stray shaft of light onto the group.

"Evening, boys," Fargo called out. "Any trouble here?"

One of the thugs glanced toward his scatter gun, propped against the building.

"Even *twitch* and you'll be looking at the wrong end of a daisy," Fargo warned.

"You needn't hold that shooter on us, mister," a second man spoke up. "This ain't a white woman—it's a Mexer."

Fargo nodded. "Hell, I reckon you boys are just having some sport."

He twirled his gun back into its holster. "Mind if I tap into that when you fellows are done?"

"We got a rule, trooper. The last man to top her has to kill her when he's done."

"Well, the price is fair enough," Fargo said, "long as I can let the pigs bury her."

Fargo could read the criminal mind as well as he could read trail sign, and he planned to let these maggots sign their own death warrants. Even now the one who had looked at his scatter-gun was edging toward the weapon. Fargo watched his drunken face contract and harden. An attempt on Fargo's life was only moments away and he set his heels—waiting, alert but calm, as he coiled for the draw.

However, he underrated his opponents. One suddenly hurled his cap into Fargo's face while the other snatched up his gun.

73

For one hair-raising instant the Trailsman faced down the twi barrels of a double-ten express gun. But the reflexes of a wil cat helped him lean far to one side just as both barrels belche yellow-orange flame.

The other two jerked back their side arms, but Fargo opene fire and drilled all three men through their lights. In case of po sum players, he reloaded and tossed a finishing shot into eac man's brain.

He calmed the girl and found out that she lived in the tir settlement of Gold Hill only a mile away. He boosted her on the Ovaro and took her home.

"*Dios le bendiga*, senor," she said, quickly kissing him b fore he handed her down.

"God bless you, too, honey," Fargo told her. "*Debes ten cu dado*. You must be more careful."

As he gigged his horse back toward Mount Davidson, Farg realized he would *need* blessing. He had just killed three regula tors in a town full of them. Suspicion would surely fall on hi because he had already publicly threatened Nash Booth's life.

"Yessir, pile on the agony," he said, causing the Ovaro's ea to prick back. "Whatever doesn't kill us, boy, can only make u stronger."

7

Fargo was sitting on the floor of Paddy Welch's flophouse, pulling on his second boot, when a well-dressed middle-aged man wearing no visible weapons stopped beside him.

"Fargo? Mr. Skye Fargo?" he asked politely.

Fargo stood up. "You have the advantage on me, Mr.—"

"Perkins. Luce Perkins."

Snake River Dan, busy tying on his wide red sash, snorted. "Just can't keep old J. Henry in your pants, can you, Skye?"

"Shut pan, you old fool," Fargo snapped. He looked at the visitor. "Sure, you're Loretta's father. Marshal Helzer tells me you're a top hand as a mining engineer. Your daughter predicted you'd be around to collect for that broken fence. It's only fair I pony up."

"What broken fence?" Perkins replied in a puzzled tone.

Dan sniggered. "Open mouth, insert foot."

"Oh," the engineer said after a moment. "Yes, I noticed that, but I didn't know you did it."

Fargo reached for his pocket, but Luce spoke up. "That damage is nothing, Mr. Fargo. Keep your money."

Fargo's brow runneled in puzzlement. "Then . . . you're warning me away from your daughter?"

"Happens you got any livestock, Perkins," Dan cut in, thoroughly enjoying all this, "best protect them, too."

Perkins sent a sharp glance at the old trapper. "A bath won't clean up your dirty mind, I suppose, but it might curb the stench blowing off you. I've been in slaughterhouses that smell better."

Snake River Dan chuckled. "Well, by God! He's a game-cock."

"It is about Loretta," Perkins continued, looking at Fargo

again, "but not what you think. She's a grown woman with emancipated ideas, and with her looks what's the use of my trying to control her actions? The cholera plague of the 'forties took her mother, and I'm too damn busy to stay home and guard her."

By now Fargo was truly confused. "But you say you're here about your daughter?"

"Absolutely. I'm terribly worried. Her life is in danger, and I was hoping—"

Luce Perkins abruptly fell silent, his smooth-shaven face turning white as gypsum. Fargo saw he was staring toward the only window. He followed Perkins' gaze and saw Septimus Dunwiddie's pasty face, Nash Booth standing beside him. Both men were staring inside at Perkins. When Fargo looked too, they moved quickly off.

"Thanks for your time," Perkins muttered, hurrying out before Fargo could even speak.

"Well, raise my rent," Dan said. "What's wrong with him and what doctor told him so?"

"Are you old *and* stupid?" Fargo shot back. "Obviously he came here for some kind of help because his daughter is in danger. Dunwiddie and Booth deliberately scared him off."

"Ahuh. He took off like a scalded dog. Seems like a nice enough jasper."

Jimmy came, armed with a Greener 12-gauge, and the three men walked to the Bluebush Café for breakfast. But thanks to repeated Indian attacks on the supply caravans from Sacramento, food supplies were suddenly critically low. A bowl of cornmeal gruel had to suffice for breakfast. While they ate, Fargo explained about the incident last night in the alley.

The trio, hands caressing their weapons, eyes to all sides, headed down Center Street toward the Wicked Sisters. At a gap between a saloon and a hardware store Fargo glanced right. The Truckee River was visible from Mount Davidson, a serpentine silver ribbon cutting through the desert a few miles north.

"Look," Fargo told his companions.

All three men saw the mirror flashes glinting along the north side of the river—the moccasin telegraph active again.

"Paiutes or Bannocks," Snake River Dan guessed. "Most

likely both. Looks like heap big doin's. But I still think you're shooting at shadows, Fargo—they ain't stupid enough to attack a settlement bristling with firearms."

"You heard Tim Bowman at the saloon," Jimmy reminded him. "Paiutes stole that gunpowder shipment for the Dundee mine."

"Hell, that's even stupider," Dan scoffed. "A Paiute don't know gunpowder from baking powder."

"What's stupid," Fargo gainsaid, "is trying to predict what any tribe will do. The red man is a notional creature. And you know for a fact that Cheyennes have invented an exploding arrow using gunpowder."

"For a surety," Dan admitted. "I plumb forgot about that. They put a blasting cap on the arrow tip and tie a little pouch of gunpowder around it. It don't always work, but they can set wagons and houses ablaze."

They moved on, Dan already trailing a reek of whiskey.

"The paleface may yet be driven out," Jimmy fretted. "I've got a kid sister named Janie back in Iowa. She's studying this new photography—wants to come out west and record the landscape. But how can I let her with savages running wild?"

"Not to mention the Indians," Fargo quipped. Jimmy's mention of his sister made Fargo worry about Loretta.

"You think the West will always be wide-open like it is now?" Jimmy asked. "You know, Indians controlling every place except the large settlements?"

Fargo shook his head. "The red aborigines are doomed just like the mountain men were. The West only looks wide-open because it's so big. But the land hunters and profiteers are already carving it up for the big bugs. You've heard how much land those spineless bootlicks in Congress are promising to the railroads—not just track bed but for huge areas bordering the tracks. And the War Department has promised timber rights to jackals who strip the land and ruin it."

"That's the straight," Jimmy agreed. "I saw it when I was a constable in Placerville. Hard-rock miners all over the Sierra are using giant hoses called dictators that wash away entire mountains in a few days. California law forbids it, but a little 'gate money' to the crooked politicians will, well, move mountains."

"Bleedin' Holy Ghost!" Snake River Dan exclaimed. "Glom that, wouldja?"

In the street just outside the Wicked Sisters, the three would-be rapists Fargo had killed the night before had been placed on display in their coffins. To rile up all the private police, the coffins were propped up at a slant against a tie rail under signs that screamed TRECHERUS MURRDUR!!!

The undertaker's lavish use of rouge and lip paint made Fargo laugh. "What a way to go out, huh? All got up like New Orleans whores."

"Pretty, innit?" Dan said. "'Cept for them holes in their skulls leakin' brain suds. You can always tell Skye Fargo's work."

Inside, the saloon was in a boil over the killings. The counter was crowded, so the new arrivals took a table and placed their backs to a wall.

"Careful, boys," Tim Bowman muttered when he brought their drinks over. "That's a special vigilance committee at the center table. Thugs from the Yellow Jacket, Savage, and Curry mines. They made their brag how they mean to hang Fargo."

"That's not very hospitable," Fargo said, blowing foam off his beer.

"Hey, Fargo!" called out a regulator in a billed cap. "You got anything to say about them bodies out front? You murdered them last night."

"'Murder' is such an ugly word, old son. Let's just say the butcher's bill was steep, eh?" He added a goading grin that made the entire group at the table scowl.

"That's *all* the hell you got to say, you back-shooting cock-chafer?"

Fargo didn't give them a smile—just a little pull of his lips. "Well, no need to mist up, Alice. You'll soon be joining your rapist friends. They need plenty of gal-boys to shovel coal in hell."

"*Now*, boys!" billed cap shouted, and suddenly four double tens came out from under the table.

"*Here's* a frolic!" Snake River Dan said joyfully, snatching both Dragoons from his sash. "Friendlies hit the deck!"

Fargo and Jimmy, too, filled their hands and crouched to fire, but before the first shot sounded, a thundering roar like a raging bull froze everyone. Out of the murky shadows near the stage,

Terrible Jack Slade emerged. His walnut-grip Remingtons seemed to spring from his holster.

"Well, now," he said to the regulators, "I see you boys are feeling sparky."

Four times the revolvers barked, producing shrieks of pain as the men, wounded in their gun hands, dropped their weapons.

"You half-faced groats are lucky," Slade told them. "I just saved your lives. You'll catch a weasel asleep before you'll kill Skye Fargo from the front."

The wounded men were in too much pain to count their blessings. They started to hustle from the saloon to find a doctor. But Jimmy suddenly surprised Fargo by training his Greener on them.

"Freeze, gentlemen, or I'll burn you down. You're all under arrest."

"For *what*, you mouthy pup?" billed cap demanded. "We're the law, too."

"In a pig's eye, Cromwell. I'm jugging you for attempted murder and for usurping federal authority. I'm a U.S. deputy, duly sworn. The moment I arrived in this city, your jurisdiction was limited to protecting the private interests of the mines employing you. Now march, and I ain't saying it twice. A doc will treat you in your cells."

"Hey, Jack," some anonymous wag called out after Jimmy left with his prisoners, "who's for supper tonight?"

Laughter bubbled through the saloon. Slade nodded ponderously. "Oh, you're *all* going to enjoy a banquet next Wednesday. Midnight sharp. I'm serving up goose cooked to a cinder."

The mood was somber now. Fargo and Snake River Dan exchanged an uneasy glance. Was a mad man, Fargo wondered, *always* crazy?

"Jack, we're obliged," Fargo said. "Lemme buy you a drink."

But before Slade could even move, a soiled dove came flying down the steps and leaped on Terrible Jack, clawing and hitting. Fargo hustled over and pulled her off.

"Simmer down, lady," he ordered her. "What's your dicker?"

"I let that filthy ape climb all over me for two hours," she protested breathlessly. "Then he took off without planking his cash. I coulda serviced ten men in that time."

"That true, Jack?"

Slade grinned slyly. "You know how it is with handsome men like us, Skye. I'd ought to charge her. She *liked* it."

"You cannibal *bastard*!" the sporting gal screeched, trying to sink her claws into Slade's eyes. Fargo restrained her, getting a few scratch marks himself.

"Jack," he said, "I sure owe you one."

Fargo reluctantly fished four gold quarter eagles from his pocket. "Will ten dollars cover it, hon?"

"No, but I'll settle for that."

Fargo returned to the table. Snake River Dan watched the indignant girl go back upstairs.

"This child would chuck all of these painted harlots," Dan opined, "for one Crow Injin gal. Beautiful women and they *do* like the old push-push."

Jimmy came back into the saloon and joined them. "You killed three regulators last night, Skye, and I just locked four more up in the calaboose. We're whittling them down."

Fargo grinned. "*That's* the gait. But we were palavering about not being able to hold men because the circuit judges can't get through. Speedy trial and all that."

"Tough titty. We also got hostile Indians painting for war. I'm declaring this an emergency and bringing Virginia City under territorial martial law. That won't require the governor's approval in Carson City."

Fargo grinned. "If you can't raise the bridge you lower the river."

"Sure, but them scum buckets got pals, sprout," Dan pointed out to Jimmy. "There's gonna be a bust out."

"Good," Fargo said. "We'll cut 'em down like yellow dogs."

"This place is a tinderbox," Jimmy said, worry in his tone. "There ain't no penknife mining here like in California. There's plenty of gold and silver, all right, but it runs in deep veins."

"The way you say," Fargo agreed. "Most of the prospectors don't understand veins."

"Yeah. As soon as they exhaust the surface ore they sell their claims for a pittance. Then they start to get boiling mad. There's hundreds of them, all stuck here. It will come to no good."

Fargo nodded. "Events have taken charge."

"We're not alone in this," Jimmy said. "See that table near the door where Bo Gramlich is sitting? Those three men with him are the prospectors I mentioned to you. Paul Robeck is the bald fellow, Billy Fredericks is wearing the sheepskin vest, and the third one is Lloyd Slaughter. All three are gun handy and willing to side us if we need them."

"Damn straight we'll need them," Fargo said.

As if timed to prove Fargo's prediction, Nash Booth and his three minions stalked in, faces distorted with rage. They crossed toward Fargo's table, but the huge bores of Snake River Dan's Dragoon pistols, hastily whipped from his sash, pulled them up short.

"Booth, you pig's afterbirth," he growled, "stand off or I'll blow two airshafts through you."

"You'll be going over the mountains soon, old man," Willard Jones said. "I'm gonna do for you just like I done for your mule."

Dan glanced at Fargo and both men grinned. Clearly Jones did not know western territorial law as well as Dan did, and Fargo rejoiced at what was coming.

"Sonny, you'll need to talk up louder," Dan said, putting a creak in his voice. "My ears has gone the way of my bladder."

"You old pus bucket, I'm *glad* I stole and killed your god-damn mule. I'm telling you I mean to kill you."

"Yep, that's what I thought you said."

The artillery roar of the Dragoon in Dan's right hand seemed obscenely loud inside the saloon. The huge ball tore into Jones' chest and blew a fist-sized hole coming out. Gobbets of flesh and lung tissue splattered the men behind him. Jones flew back five feet, dead before he hit the ground like a sack of dirt.

Booth, Chilly Davis, and Sam Watson suddenly looked as if they'd been drained by leeches.

Snake River Dan wagged his guns. "Any of you chicken-plucking sons of bucks want the balance of these pills?"

"*Murder!*" Booth shouted. "Marshal, lock that son of a bitch up!"

Jimmy shook his head. "I can't," he said matter-of-factly. "In the territories, a direct threat on a man's life is an imminent danger. Dan had every right."

"Yeah, that's the usual hokum when Fargo's around, ain't it?"

Fargo laughed. He placed his hand on the butt of his Colt.

"How 'bout you, child scalper? You feel like announcing any plans to kill me?"

Booth opened his mouth but wisely swallowed back his first response. "That's mighty thin, Fargo, just like your pecker."

Loud and derisive female laughter greeted this remark. Fargo saw Smooth Bore and Tit Bit watching from the stairs.

"Nash," Smooth Bore taunted, "my girls have told me about that tiny tallywhacker of yours. You're a mole hill talking to a mountain."

The saloon exploded in raucous laughter and jeers. Infuriated and abjectly humiliated, Nash stomped out, Davis and Watson dragging the corpse.

Dan tossed back a shot of whiskey. "Damn but that was great larks. Told you I'd do for that bastard."

"I never doubted it, old son," Fargo assured him. "You're a good man to take along."

Conversation was interrupted by a fast drumroll as the troupe of acrobats, magicians, and jugglers filed onto the stage at the back of the saloon. Fargo marveled at their talent as he watched a magician called Merlin pour a pitcher of water into his hat, then clap it on a customer's head completely dry.

"Tarnal hell!" Dan exclaimed. "I ain't never seen the like."

Fargo slowly nodded, Dan's words sparking a vague idea. "I wonder . . ."

"Wonder what?"

Fargo thought of the mirror flashes earlier. "How many ways there are to skin a cat," he replied.

"Bring me the white-eye seller of strong water," the Paiute medicine man Sis-ki-dee ordered one of his Sash Warriors. "And tell Eagle On His Journey to bring one of his best dogs forward when the sun has moved the distance of one lodge pole."

Sis-ki-dee and the war chief Plenty Coups stood at the far edge of the barren desert camp. The fingernails adorning the shaman's buckskin leggings were pale and opaque in the late afternoon sunshine.

"I have told you many times," Sis-ki-dee said, "there are ways to kill besides foolishly standing in front of the white devils' thunder sticks. Now the dogs are well trained to hate the white-man smell. You will see how it is with your own eyes."

Plenty Coups, who took great pride in never showing his feelings in his face as women and white men did, nonetheless scowled in disapproval.

"I have ears, Contrary Warrior, when you say we must attack," he said. "But it is not the Warrior Way to kill without counting coup and—"

"Then join the women in their sewing lodge," Sis-ki-dee cut him off sharply. "Things are the way they are—do you not see it? Why push if a thing won't move? All the world knows you are a brave and deadly fighter, a man fit to wear the buffalo horns in battle. Your coup feathers trail on the ground. But these white invaders are true spawn of the Windigo, and now a 'noble' Paiute is a dead Paiute."

"You speak words a brave can place in his parfleche," Plenty Coups finally said.

"As you say. And do not forget that your brave warriors *will* face the enemy and kill them. But they are like a plague of locusts, too many to fight with our small numbers. Our white prisoner has told me how to use the big-thundering powder we have captured. We—"

The Sash Warrior arrived just then with a prisoner in tow, a thin, frightened, badly burned and scarred whiskey peddler who had foolishly tried to cross the wrong stretch of desert.

Sis-ki-dee had learned some English during his days in the Green River country. "You are fortunate, white dog. I decide to let you go. The white man's lodge circle lies straight west from here. Take this."

Sis-ki-dee handed the man a bladder bag of water. "You can walk there in less than one sleep."

"Juh-Juh-Jesus," the astounded captive stammered. "Thank you, Chief."

Sis-ki-dee suddenly reached out and ripped a piece from the prisoner's butternut-dyed shirt. The captive looked startled, but Sis-ki-dee's deep panther scars made his face terrible to behold as did the insane sheen of his black obsidian eyes. The white man wisely held his tongue.

"Well?" Sis-ki-dee demanded. "Will you stand there blubbering until I gut you?"

The whiskey peddler required no further encouragement. Limping, but moving rapidly, he bore off across the hot white sand toward the miragelike silhouette of Mount Davidson, an image rippling in the heat.

The two Paiutes watched him recede like a figure in a dream disappearing in a long tunnel.

"Eagle On His Journey will be here soon," Sis-ki-dee said. "Catch up one of your ponies."

Both braves were mounted when Eagle On His Journey arrived holding a savage-fanged yellow cur on a braided rope. Indians were famous for raising vicious sentry dogs, but Sis-ki-dee had made sure the camp pack were also attack weapons.

He tossed the scrap of shirt to the new arrival. "You know what to do."

The brave rubbed the cloth against the cur's muzzle while cuffing and swatting the animal's nose. The mongrel quivered in fury, eager to seize its quarry. Eagle On His Journey untied the rope, and the dirty yellow killing machine was off like an arrow from the bow.

The two Paiutes heeled their ponies in pursuit. Soon they could see the white man's desperate face as he looked back at the pursuing cur. He tried to run, but his ordeal in the Indian camp had left him too weak. He tripped, sprawled headlong, and tried to struggle to his feet.

The next instant the dog leaped on him in a snarling rage, and the man's screams shattered the eerie desert silence.

Plenty Coups looked astounded as the cur went straight for the man's throat, literally ripping it out like the heart from a buffalo. The scream ceased and the dying man's heels scratched the dirt a few times in death agony.

"Now do you doubt we can attack the white skins?" Sis-ki-dee boasted. "First we send in the dog packs, at various places in their lodge town, to panic and distract them. While this goes on, we sneak in with the big-thundering powder and kill as many as we can and start many fires. Then you will lead your Sash Warriors in to kill the remainder—and yes, to count coup first."

Plenty Coups, still staring as the half-starved dog tore out the dead man's glistening vitals, finally seemed convinced.

"I have ears. The Bannocks under Chief Yellow Bear will join us as they did at Weeping Woman Lake," he said, meaning the place white-eyes called Pyramid Lake. "And perhaps Medicine Flute, the Shoshone Contrary Warrior, will bring his band down from north of the Washoe. It will be another great victory just like Weeping Woman."

Sis-ki-dee's soulless eyes looked toward the distant mountain where, even now, the foolish and greedy white men were scratching glittering yellow rocks from the earth.

"No, brother," he corrected, "not *just* like. The Paiute winter count will record our greatest victory ever. For *this* time we will kill many, many more. So many that they will never invade our land again."

8

The sun was a dull red ball disappearing behind the ermine capes of the Sierra Nevada when Fargo rode downslope toward Raisin Street and the one relatively peaceful section of Virginia City.

He was supposed to be patrolling for signs of vigilante activity, but the image of Loretta Perkins had become like a catchy tune he couldn't shake from his mind. She had teased him twice now, and it was time to fish or cut bait—and Fargo was an experienced fisherman. But even if he couldn't slip under her lilac-scented petticoats, at least he could talk to her father about that mysterious visit to Paddy Welch's place this morning. Clearly Luce Perkins believed his daughter was in danger—and just as clearly, Nash Booth and Septimus Dunwiddie were behind the trouble.

He slowed the Ovaro to a walk as he reached the two-story house where Loretta and her father lived. Lights blazed in most of the downstairs windows and Fargo grinned when he saw the still-broken picket fence. He swung down and led the Ovaro into the carriage way, hobbling him foreleg to rear in the protective shadows.

He banged the heavy brass knocker on the front door.

"Who is it?" Loretta's guarded voice called out.

"I'm the third button on a two-button vest, as your bodyguard put it."

The door swung open and Fargo was face-to-face with a true breathtaking beauty. Loretta wore a pretty lavender muslin dress with a princess lace collar. Her finely sculpted cheekbones were framed by twin waterfalls of shining brown hair. The long hallway behind her was lighted by wall lamps in tin reflectors, the soft light making her glow like an angel's halo.

She gave him a coy glance he could feel in his hip pocket. "Something on your mind, Mr. Fargo?"

"Plenty. Is your father home?"

She looked surprised at his answer. "He was forced to work late at the mine. Something about a broken pump. Would you like to come in?"

Fargo hesitated, knowing the rules governing unchaperoned "good girls."

"You needn't look so blasé," she bristled.

"What the hell does that mean? I just don't think I should come in the front door, is all. It doesn't take much to ruin a girl's reputation, not with a man like me. Matter fact, I've ruined a few."

Her color heightened noticeably. "I see you're honest but tactless. And you're right. You can leave your horse out back and come in through the kitchen door."

Fargo did as she suggested and joined her in a high-ceilinged kitchen with an iron cookstove and two big wooden sinks.

"I take it you know there's an antelope in your backyard?" he said.

"Yes, but I've tamed him. You can pet him just like a dog."

Fargo grinned. "Yeah, he ran right up to me. That's impressive—an antelope is a mighty skittish animal."

She held his gaze, a smile dancing on her lips. "I'm good with wild things, Skye."

Fargo glanced around. "Don't tell me you're alone in this big house," he added.

"Yes, more's the pity. Unlike back home, no ladies' maid, no housemaid, and no cook but an old Chinese woman who dips snuff and serves fish heads and rice."

Fargo propped his rifle against a wall. "That's not exactly what I mean, pretty lady. Isn't your bodyguard around?"

She pulled her right hand into view and Fargo saw the .36 Colt Navy. "For some mysterious reason he quit. And no matter what wages Father offers, we can't find another one. So I carry this at all times."

"I suspect the reason isn't mysterious at all, is it?"

"Perhaps not. But I'm not alone in the house now, am I?"

She led Fargo into a comfortable parlor featuring a Persian

rug, a sofa with a serpentine back, and chairs with crocheted doilies for head and armrests.

Fargo whistled. "Mighty high-toned."

"Yes. It was shipped in from California before the serious Indian troubles began. Now we're lucky if we can get a few plates. And I suppose I'll never see the watered silk ball dress I ordered from Sacramento."

"Seems to me you've got bigger problems than a lack of ball gowns."

She cast her eyes downward and said nothing. The two of them sat down side by side on a little love seat, Loretta smoothing her dress with both hands. Fargo tugged the square of scented lace handkerchief from her right sleeve and sniffed it.

"Hmm . . . hyacinth. Very nice."

"Well, you're familiar with *some* of the nicer things in life, I see."

He laughed, stroking her soft hair. "Do you think that a man who wears buckskins can't tell an opera from a medicine show?"

"*Think?* Thoughts will not always submit to a master—especially when *you* are in the room."

"That sounds promising to me," he said, "but you're good at putting up a smoke screen with words. Is there any fire behind your smoke?"

He answered his own question by enfolding her in his arms and kissing those glistening, cherry red lips. Her responding fire was immediate as her tongue explored his mouth and her breathing grew more rapid.

"Answer your question?"

"In spades," he assured her. "But I got one more."

"That being . . . ?"

"Last time we talked you made a big show out of letting me know you'd never dally with any man who took on two women at once. What changed your mind?"

She ran the tip of her tongue over her lips. "That's easy. I started wondering *what* a man who could please two women at once must be like when he's with just one."

Loretta nodded toward a decanter on a little taboret beside Fargo. "Sherry and bitters?"

Fargo shook his head. "I like my liquor to kick."

"Well," she said, fluttering her long lashes at him, "we seem to have run out of small talk. May I be bold?"

He grinned. "One of us better be, and it's your house."

"Yes, well . . ."

She plucked a buttonhook from the taboret and began to free the buttons on the sides of her shoes. "I had just finished heating water for a bath when you arrived. Care to join me?"

"A fellow can't be too clean, can he?"

She looked askance at his buckskins. "Apparently not. Are those bloodstains on the fringes?"

"Animal," he assured her, leaving it there.

"It's a courteous lie, so I'll forgive you."

Fargo tugged off her silk-lined shoes, pulling her up from the love seat.

She took his hand and led him to a small room off the kitchen, dominated by an oval claw-foot tub made of iron. Wraiths of steam still rose from the water.

"It's hot," she warned as the Trailsman's deft fingers began to loosen the stays of her bodice. She laughed. "I see you've undressed women before."

"Every chance I get," he admitted.

"Good. *I'll* profit from that experience." While she spoke she pulled out her tortoiseshell hairpins. "A woman does not fall in love with a man like you. With you it must be an *amour*, a brief and illicit love."

In fact, Fargo had no interest in the love part, but the "brief" appealed to him. So did this wasp-waisted beauty's top-shelf body. He tugged off her dress and chemise, then slid down her frilly step-ins, feeling blood plunge into his manhood at the sight of her. The tiny waist flared into wide hips, and her coffee-colored mons bush looked lush and exciting against the porcelain skin. He made her shudder almost violently when he cupped her hard tits and sucked each nipple stiff while one finger worked her pearl nubbin until it swelled out of its chamois hood.

"Oh, now *you* get naked," she moaned. "You're reminding me how much I need a man inside me."

Fargo unbuckled his shell belt and hung it on a wooden wall peg. In jig time his clothes were a puddle on the floor. In spite of herself she couldn't help staring at his rigid member, so stiff the tip was purple with engorged blood.

"My stars, Skye. You are certainly . . . well equipped."

"And sound in wind and limb," he assured her. "Let's test the waters."

It was too hot, but a bucket of cold water sitting nearby tempered it. Fargo swung in first, then guided her onto his lap.

"Careful, that's dynamite with the fuse burning," he warned her when Loretta began stroking his turgid manhood. Pleasure jolted along its length and caused a tingling tightness in his groin.

"Good," she said, "because I plan to make it explode hard."

She spoke close into his ear, her breath animal warm. "Skye," she said in a voice made throaty from lust, "most men hold back with me thinking I am too fragile. They are wrong. Tonight we will shame the delicate. And I warn you—I am loud."

"Whatever floats your boat, girl," he said, not really giving a damn for all this talk. He lined himself up with her nether portal and flexed his hips hard to plunge deep inside her.

The cry of abandon she loosed, as the walls of her sex stretched wide to accommodate him, made Fargo flinch even in the throes of pleasure.

"Easy, girl," he coaxed. "You'll scare the antelope."

He switched from pliant nipple to pliant nipple like a metronome, biting just hard enough to increase her frenzy as he drove his length rapidly in and out. Water sloshed noisily over the lip of the tub as the wave motion increased.

"Oh, merciful saints!" she cried out. "Skye, what . . . *oh!* What are you *doing* to . . . oh! Oh! *OHH!*"

The tub began to rock as a hard, fast string of climaxes exploded inside her, a cresting wave that made her lose control of her body. Fargo had to grip her pearl-smooth ass hard to keep her from bouncing out onto the floor. He went into the strong finish, taking her over the sun one more time with him.

They both sprawled, dead to the world, until the water cooled and Fargo's drifting mind recalled that Luce Perkins might come home at any time. After they had toweled off and begun dressing, he asked her bluntly: "Loretta, why would your father believe your life is in danger?"

She didn't even flinch at the question. "I don't know for sure. Something is happening between him and Septimus Dunwiddie, I think, because Father sure does curse him lately."

"Dunwiddie, huh? Then it has to have something to do with getting his hands on Ephraim Cole's Schofield mine."

"I think so, too," she said as she laced the stays of her bodice. "But father did tell me that he's sure Nash Booth and some other thugs employed by the mines have formed a pact to kill you."

Fargo's strong white teeth flashed through his beard when he grinned. "I wouldn't have it any other way. After all, I been killing them and I plan to kill more."

As arranged, Fargo rendezvoused with Snake River Dan and Jimmy at the jailhouse.

"Step out front, boys," he called to his friends from the doorway, not wanting the prisoners to hear them talking.

"Step on a cat's tail, Fargo!" shouted Cromwell, a thug from the Yellow Jacket. "Your ass is grass. All three of you crusading sons of bitches will soon be barking in hell!"

"Whatever you say," Fargo replied amiably. "Hell, who am I to doubt a bravo like you?"

"The hell you been?" Dan demanded of the Trailsman after Jimmy shut the door. "I didn't see you patrolling—"

Dan fell silent, getting a good whiff of the perfume wafting off Fargo. "Fargo, you hound, you are some pumpkins. You was diddlin' that Perkins gal, eh?"

"It's none of your picnic, Methuselah. You don't even get it up anymore unless you're piss-proud in the morning."

"Huh! *This* child's fires ain't banked yet."

Fargo looked at Jimmy in the near darkness. "I thought those prospectors were coming here to help you guard that trash? Seems likely their friends will try a bust out."

"They're coming well heeled and they'll sleep all night in the jailhouse," Jimmy confirmed. "I sent 'em to the Bluebush for some grub. They'll be back quick."

"Good. I'm worried about the signs of Indian activity so close to town. They might have a nasty surprise for us, and it might be something besides that stolen black powder. Me and His Mulishness here are riding out to take a squint around that Paiute camp in the desert southeast of town."

"Fargo, at least pre-*tend* you got more brains than a rabbit," Dan sputtered. "Since when did topping a pretty gal turn you stupid?"

"Stow it. I said I'd get you killed, and by the Lord Harry I will."

Jimmy said, "You think that's a wise play, Skye? Riding out to the Paiute camp, I mean. You yourself said those are no boys to fool with."

"Wise? Hell no. I'd rather shove a wolverine down my pants. But I've learned the hard way to scout an enemy before I have to fight him. These red sons in Nevada ain't cracker-and-molasses Indians growing gardens on a rez. They've signed no treaties and they never will. We need to know what they're up to."

Jimmy snapped his fingers. "Say! Billy Fredericks left a little something in your saddlebag earlier. You were asking about it— might come in handy tonight."

"Strangers headed our way," Dan warned. "Be ready for a set-to."

"It's all right," Jimmy said. "It's just Paul, Billy, and Lloyd coming back from their meal."

Fargo greeted the three prospectors with a handshake and thanked them for their help. The three new arrivals, armed with revolvers and scatterguns, went inside. The jailhouse stood at the eastern edge of town, and Fargo spotted a shadowy figure coming up the moonlit slope on foot.

"Fade, boys," he muttered to his friends. "The size on that hombre tells me that's Terrible Jack Slade."

All three men ducked into an alley between the jailhouse and the dry goods store next door, now closed for business. Slade moved past as if in a trance, muttering something to himself that Fargo couldn't hear.

"He's shorely out on the roof tonight," Dan whispered. "Drunk and crazy."

Fargo nodded. "We best see where he goes. Next Wednesday is creeping up on us. If he's telling the straight, we got only four days until . . . whatever's coming."

He looked at the marshal. "Jimmy, you're the law around here and this is your bailiwick. So all three of us should go."

The three men moved into the wide and dusty street on foot, staying near the plank-board walk but avoiding traffic in the street. Slade, however, stayed to the middle of the road, forcing horse-backers to swing around him.

"He didn't go in the Wicked Sisters," Jimmy remarked. "That's usually where he drinks."

Yellow light, drunken voices, and piano music spilled from one watering hole after another, but Slade walked straight ahead like a hound on point. Soon the raucous town lay behind the three men, and they were headed down the western slope of Mount Davidson under a buttery full moon.

"Ah, hell," Dan finally said. "He ain't goin' nowheres special. You turds know he's crazy as a coot. Let's give it up as a bad job. I hate travelin' shank's mare—I got a bunion the size of a melon."

"He does like to wander aimlessly at night," Jimmy confirmed. "I've followed him for hours to no purpose."

"Fine," Fargo replied, "but after the threat he's made, wouldn't it be smart to dog his heels?"

"That shines," Dan agreed reluctantly. "But we best be damn careful. When he's been dippin' his beak in Old Churnbrain he's meaner 'n a badger in a barrel."

"That's fine by me," Fargo said grimly. "Let him strike at us. I got a God-fear it's not just all talk this time. He's up to something deucedly wicked—and it just might be time to kill him for the good of the many."

"*Now* you're whistlin'," Dan approved, tugging out his Dragoons. "I'll air him out right-ass now."

"As you were," Jimmy snapped. "This is *my* town even if I ain't got it under control, and there'll be no outright murder if I can help it. Skye said let him strike at us first. It has to be self-defense."

Fargo chuckled. "The lad's right, lunkhead."

"Ah, Jimmy's fresh out of three-corner britches. He's still mad about that rattlesnake trick I played. But I reckon he's right," Dan added. "Murder in front of a marshal is like screwin' in front of a preacher."

"Damn," Fargo said, "he just jogged off the freight road. Hurry up or we'll lose him."

They angled off the road and turned the shoulder of the mountain. Below in the moonlight, located in the crotch of two narrow gulches, was a huge rock tumble abutting the Schofield mine. Light was generous, but Slade was nowhere to be seen.

"He's gone," Jimmy said.

Fargo nodded. "Gone quick. Like a fist when you open your hand. He has to be in those rocks somewhere."

Fargo shucked out his Colt and palmed the wheel to check the action. "Let's take a look, but fill your hands first. You saw how quick he tagged those curly wolves in the saloon."

The three men crept up to the rocks, Fargo fully aware of how dangerous Slade could be. They began a careful search behind each rock. But a half-hour search was fruitless.

"He ain't here," Dan finally said. "He can't be."

Fargo was inclined to agree. But how had he slipped away?

The words were sudden and unexpected, coming from behind Fargo. "Did you boys lose something?"

"Katy Christ!" Snake River Dan exclaimed while Jimmy nearly jumped out of his boots. Fargo, too, felt a jolt of cool shock.

He turned around. Slade was an imposing figure in the moonlight, wild and handsome and menacing. His silver belt gleamed like quicksilver.

"Evening, Jack," Fargo greeted him. "How did you get behind us? We searched the spot where you're standing."

"I was on the ground getting ready to sleep."

"Sleep? Out here?"

"Sure. You know I have a surfeit of enemies, Skye. Sometimes I take a nap out here where it's safe."

"You have enemies, all right," Fargo said, "but they're all scared to death of you."

Slade laughed hard as if Fargo had told a good dirty story. "Skye, I rent a flimsy lean-to off of Hubbard's butcher shop. It ain't even got a door. It takes no great ration of guts to do for a man in his sleep."

"Mm. So these rocks have got nothing to do with whatever you say is coming at midnight Wednesday?"

Again Slade laughed, a hyenalike bark that grated like a rasp on Fargo's nerves. "Oh, *that*. No, sir."

"Is that all of it, Jack?" Jimmy added.

"Every Gospel."

Fargo didn't buy it. A man Slade's size was hard to overlook, yet Fargo had searched carefully.

"But the Wrath *is* coming," Slade added. "Yessir, the omnipotent Wrath."

Slade let loose with a fiery tirade about the mark of the Beast, making no sense that Fargo could discern. Then he finally gave his "preaching" a pulpit pause.

"Jack," Fargo said, "what's going to happen next Wednesday?"

"What *won't* happen? Yessir, screwed, glued, and tattooed. The whole mother-humpin' city."

"Now you don't sound like a preacher—just a murderer."

"Too late to reform me. I've already killed twenty-seven men."

Fargo wasn't eager for a draw-shoot with this inveterate killer. But he was nearly convinced by now that Slade wasn't bluffing about next Wednesday. Sometimes a man had to choose the lesser evil.

Fargo twirled his six-gun back into its holster. "Care to try making it twenty-eight men, Jack?"

"You mean you want a showdown?"

"Want it? No. But you're threatening to kill me and everybody else in four days, so I'd just as soon lock horns now. Man to man, not sneaking around in the shadows."

Slade stubbornly shook his head. "I won't mix it up with you for two reasons: I like you and I'm afraid you might kill me. If you three want me dead, you'll have to murder me."

Slade nonchalantly stretched out on the hard ground between two boulders and pulled his hat over his eyes. "Night, gents."

9

"So you don't want no murder on your watch, huh, Jimmy?" Snake River Dan said, his tone heavy with disgust. "The *Wrath* is coming, my hairy white ass. That son of a bitch is playing us like a fiddle."

The three friends were climbing the westward slope of Mount Davidson, heading back toward town.

"I'm going to scour those rocks real careful in daylight," Jimmy vowed. "He disappeared and reappeared like some ghost, but we searched everywhere."

"That moonstruck bastard sure's hell wasn't hiding," Dan agreed. "I'll help you search, Jimmy boy."

"He wasn't hiding above the ground," Fargo corrected his friend.

"Say, that shines," Jimmy agreed. "We'll have to look for a tunnel or something."

"Well, we still have four days," Fargo said. "Right now, Dan, we've got to scout that Paiute camp. That's trouble brewing. Especially if they figure out how gunpowder works—assuming that's what they got in mind."

"Why can't I ride out with you?" Jimmy demanded.

"Because at your age a man is like a three-year-old colt, that's why. Old enough to have your strength but not enough good sense. Are you really going to leave those three prospectors to guard *your* prisoners? I took you along here because it's a town matter, but Indians are not subject to white man's laws. You're needed here in your town."

Jimmy loosed a long sigh. "Yeah, you're right. This town's cram-full of bullyboys. Besides, why would frontiersmen like you want to take a kid who can't even pour pee out of a boot?"

"H'ar now!" Dan scoffed. "Nobody said no such thing. There's green on your antlers, mebbe, but *this* child says you're a good man to ride the river with."

"It took sand to accept a lawman's job on the Comstock," Fargo chimed in. "We're counting on you, Marshal, and you just wait—you *will* prove your mettle. Matter fact, you did it yesterday when you arrested those hired guns in the saloon."

Jimmy peeled off at the jailhouse and Fargo and Dan continued on to the livery barn. They knew that if their mounts foundered back of beyond both men would end up suffering days of excruciating torture if Paiutes or Bannocks caught them. So, working in the light of a coal-oil lamp, they used hoof-picks to pry loose any small stones from their horses' hooves and then checked them carefully for stone bruises and hairline cracks.

They tacked their mounts, checked their weapons, then rode out of town to the east. A full moon and cloudless sky made for near-daylight conditions in the white-sand desert.

"This is a fine warhorse," Fargo said of the Ovaro, "but times like this I fret his white markings. You know what Indian camps are like—they got no 'bedtime.'"

"Hell no. Wunst I stayed the night at a friendly Cheyenne camp near Powder River. Why, them red sons is dog eaters. A fat puppy is a real whatchacallit—delicacy to them. They stayed up all night bilin' a passel of 'em, tossing in rose hips for seasoning."

"The word Cheyenne means 'dog eaters,' you fool. Well, did you eat any?"

Snake River Dan, riding on Fargo's left, shrugged. "When in Rome . . . it was tolerable. I been forced to eat prairie dog a few times, and *there's* a greasy mess that's hard to swallow."

Fargo reined in. It hadn't taken them long to reach the area where it was dangerous to wander alone or straggle by day—and for riders with white skin it was double dangerous after dark. Fargo swung down and felt the ground lightly with three fingertips.

"I can't feel any riders close by," he said as he forked leather and gigged the Ovaro forward. "But that doesn't mean they won't be out there. From what I hear of this shaman Sis-ki-dee, he's good at making braves ignore the old taboos like not leaving camp at night."

"Now, see, that's what I don't savvy. Being as how it's so

hard to fake magic, why do so many of these big-medicine men keep making so many jackleg promises about arrows that can't miss and bullets that turn into sand?"

"I'm hanged if I can puzzle out that one. Almost every time some big medicine fails, the shaman is killed. They seek a vision, and some of them chew on peyote and such. And don't forget that most red men are notional and superstitious. Sis-ki-dee, *if* he's with this bunch, will have something up his sleeve to make sure he doesn't fail."

"Happens Paiutes do hit the warpath," Dan said, "seems likely there'll be Bannocks with them."

"The way you say. And that's a vigorous and cruel tribe."

A moment later they dismounted and led their horses through a sandy wash to lessen the strain on their narrow ankles. There was absolutely no reference point in this open vastness, and Fargo checked the dawn star in the east to orient them.

"H'ar now," Dan grumbled at his horse. "Quit that damn fake limp, you bucket of glue. You'll get mescal back in town."

They moved forward at a trot, Fargo's eyes sweeping the terrain, his ears attuned for any noise that didn't belong. The butt plate of his Henry rested on his thigh, the weapon pointing straight up.

Dan lowered his voice to a hoarse whisper. "Fargo?"

"Yeah?"

"J'ever wonder . . . what the hell does a buzzard eat for dessert?"

Fargo glanced over at him. "You soft-brained fool, this ain't no Sunday stroll. Shut pan and stay alert. You won't see buzzards out here anyhow."

They rode for perhaps another five minutes when a grisly sight materialized straight ahead: a severed human head on a pike.

"Tender Virgin!" Dan whispered when they had ridden closer. "That's Micah Young, the whiskey peddler from Carson City. His whole darn gullet's been ripped out."

Fargo dismounted and knelt in the desert sand, moving carefully about and peering close in the generous moon wash to study the sign without disturbing it. "Micah here was running for his life on foot, judging from the distance between prints. A dog or wolf caught him."

"Ain't no wolves in this part of the territory. No good hunting for 'em."

Fargo nodded. "Most likely it was one of the yellow curs favored by Indians. And it was sicced on him—I see the prints of two unshod ponies. Indian dogs are trained to be vicious—I once saw one kill a gray wolf."

Fargo stood up, peering uneasily across the reflecting sand. "The ground dips up ahead—we could be close to their camp and not even know it. If we're detected moving in, we'll have to light a shuck outta here in a puffin' hurry. No Paiute wants to die without his horse nearby. That leaves him without a mount in the Land of Ghosts. One mistake and they'll be on us quicker 'n scat."

"That ain't all of it, neither," Dan replied as both men hit leather. "These far-west Injins like to keep a special running horse just for the chase."

"My stallion can outrun a lightning bolt," Fargo bragged, "then stop on a dime and give you a nickel in change. That drunken nag of yours will require a shot and a beer before he runs."

Dan chuckled. "God's truth. I'll be better off afoot."

Fargo enforced strict silence as they moved in closer, and when he heard the voices of children at play he signaled Dan to light down. They led their horses onward, Fargo keeping his stallion in the lead and making sure they were upwind of camp—Indians rarely kept sentries out and didn't need to thanks to their vigilant curs.

The Ovaro suddenly froze in place and gave his trouble snort, pawing at the ground. Fargo hissed at Dan to stop. He folded to his knees and studied the ground.

"Crude pitfall traps," he whispered. "I'd wager they ring the camp. This bunch ain't here to weave blankets."

"Is the game worth the candle?" Dan wondered. "Mebbe we best reverse our dust?"

"Well, that's sensible, and I won't call you a coward if you do. But I'm going closer. I still say this bunch has a trick up their sleeves or they wouldn't be riding so close to Virginia City. There's an attack coming."

"Hell, I can only die wunst, and you're determined to get my life over," the old trapper groused.

Both men advanced forward with caution, using the Ovaro as

their bellwether. They paused at the lip where the desert plateau formed a ridge, getting a good view of the firelit camp below. Fargo estimated about two hundred wickiups and a few bigger lodges, hardly sufficient numbers to attack Virginia City unless plenty of Bannocks and Shoshones joined them as they had at the Pyramid Lake Uprising.

As he had expected, the camp was still active. Children chased each other around, shooting miniature arrows from tiny bows. Like white men, Indians were enthusiastic gamblers, and some huddled around fires playing dice with animal teeth. Others were wagering on footraces or wrestling contests.

"Look at that big he-bear standing off by hisself," Dan whispered. "The one with the scarred face and his arms covered with brassards. Mighten that be Sis-ki-whosis?"

Fargo pulled out his spyglasses and focused them while he studied the ominous-looking brave.

"It sure's hell is Sis-ki-dee," he confirmed. "His leggings are covered with fingernails. Won't be long and hell *will* be a-poppin' in Virginia City. And look at that big dog pen they've built just south of camp—does that seem jake to you?"

"Don't make sense to me nohow. I ain't never been to no Indian camp where the dogs ain't running loose. That's how they get the most pertection outta them."

Fargo nodded. "And look at the numbers. That explains why there's no dead horses after all these raids in the area—they're feeding horse meat to the dogs. They've likely penned them because they're trained to be even more vicious than usual. And we just saw what one of those curs can do."

"Moses on the mountain! And there must be, hell, near a hundred dogs in that pen."

"Mm. Not enough to attack and defeat a big settlement, but enough to raise hell and distract the residents," Fargo speculated. He studied the camp for a minute in intent silence.

"Why two guards on that big lodge at the far edge of camp?" he wondered.

"Prisoners?"

"Could be," Fargo said, "but even prisoners would likely have a fire pit inside so the Paiutes could see they're still there."

"Mebbe that black powder," Dan suggested.

"That would explain not having a fire. I got no choice but to go down and try to look."

"Christ, Fargo, are you daft? There's guards."

"Yeah, but they're bored to dickens. That one in the bone breastplate has wandered off to get a better glom of the races. Maybe I can get close enough to the second one to conk him on the cabeza—it looks like he's about to nod out."

"It's your funeral," Dan whispered back. "Well, best give me your reins to hold."

"Like hell. If the alarm goes up, I'll never get away on foot. It's each man for himself, Dan. If they commence to whooping and yipping, just haul your bacon back to Virginia City."

Fargo dared not cut through the camp, so he hooked north leading the Ovaro and then swung to the east, keeping the camp at a distance of about fifty yards. The wind was variable tonight, which bothered him because of the dogs, but right now it blew out of the southwest.

Fargo drew up behind the lodge and threw the reins forward to hold his horse in place. Suddenly a child, perhaps tagged by a miniature arrow, shrieked loudly and Fargo pinched the Ovaro's nostrils shut to keep him from whinnying.

The Trailsman left his Henry in its saddle scabbard and picked up a good-size rock from the desert floor. He cat-footed closer to the lodge, abruptly aware when the wind quit blowing against the right side of his face—and shifted to his back.

The fat's in the fire, Fargo told himself.

The pandemonium was almost instantaneous. The dogs sent up a snarling, barking racket that ignited war whoops from the Paiutes. Feeling the fine hairs on his nape stiffen, Fargo sprinted back to the Ovaro. A stone-tipped lance missed Fargo by inches when the closest guard spotted him.

The guard shrieked a warning, and Fargo might have died on the spot if Snake River Dan hadn't violated the order about saving his own skin. Knowing Fargo was up against it, the old codger shouted, "Hell's a-poppin, featherheads!" and begun blasting at the camp with his powerful Colt Dragoons. These loud pistols were nearly as intimidating as the greatly feared "big-talking guns" or field howitzers used by the U.S. Army.

The camp was thrown into a milling panic, but not the brave

still hurtling toward Fargo in a kill fury, obsidian knife in his hand. Fargo had no choice now—it was kill or be killed. He plucked the Arkansas toothpick from its boot sheath and threw it in a fast overhand toss, driving the blade deep into the charging warrior's chest. Momentum carried the Paiute another few feet forward before he fell skidding to the ground face-first.

Fargo rolled him over and placed one foot on his chest to jerk the knife out. He wiped it on the dead brave's legging and returned to the Ovaro, knowing it wouldn't be long before Dan ran out of loads and the frightened Paiutes turned lethal again.

But Fargo did not fork leather and spur his mount. He realized that, after this botched mission, no white man would ever get near that lodge again. Whatever was inside, humans or weapons, would have to be dealt with now. He plunged a hand into his offside saddle pocket and emerged with the stick of dynamite Billy Fredericks had obtained for him.

A few lucifers wrapped in oilskin could mean a chance to live when there was no time for flint and steel. Fargo plucked one from his possibles bag then scratched it to life and ignited the fuse on the dynamite. He flipped it toward the back of the lodge and vaulted into the saddle.

"Fade, Dan!" he roared. "Fire in the hole!"

Fargo didn't need to heel the Ovaro. His savvy stallion leapt into motion as if spring-loaded. One item Fargo only suspected to be inside that lodge was copious amounts of black powder. Ten seconds later, however, when the entire world seemed to go crack-booming around him in a brilliant flash of light, he realized how wrong he was.

The explosive concussion almost knocked him from the saddle. Lodge poles took off like dangerous rockets, and stones and sand slapped into his back like buckshot. It would have been an impressive detonation even for a Comstock demolition team, but here in the open desert, among Indians who rarely witnessed such things, it was the very arrival of the Windigo himself.

Fargo doubted that many had been seriously hurt, and hoped he was right—every man had a right to face an attacker in a fair contest, and red men were no exception. He had no quarrel with this bunch and regretted having to kill the guard. But it was likely he had saved many more lives by destroying that powder.

Most of the Paiutes he could see were in no mood for a

chase. Some lay prostrate with fear at this thunder magic; others were fleeing south on foot into the open desert. Ahead on the moonlit desert plane Fargo saw Snake River Dan's skewbald streaking to the west.

The Trailsman gave the Ovaro a few cuts across the flanks with his hat, fading into the dark maw of the night.

10

Snake River Dan quaffed his warm beer and chuckled. "Fargo, by God! You brought the thunder down on them featherheads last night. When that black powder went up they was *all* clutchin' their medicine bags and praying to the Day Maker."

"I damn near got religion, too," Fargo replied. "And if it hadn't blown up, I'm thinking both of us would he hanging upside down over hot fire right about now. I must be losing my touch, old son, to alert the entire camp."

"Ah, bottle it. No man can control the wind. Wunst it went agin you, you done everything right. We're here, ain't we?"

Fargo cast a quick glance around the cavernous interior of the Wicked Sisters. Though it was nearly noon, the place was only sparsely occupied, and he saw no one who looked like a private deputy.

"Gloat all you like," he said. "We did *not* put the kibosh on the Indian threat. Sure, we ruined the black powder, and that's good. But no tribe lets it go when their camp is invaded."

"Ahuh, I know that. The red man holds a grudge until it hollers mama. So does Snake River Dan—Willard Jones found that out."

"Where's Jimmy?" Fargo inquired.

"That young pup is still searching the rocks where Terrible Jack went last night. This hoss helped him for two hours, but wunst the dew dried off it got hot 'nuff to sunburn a horny toad."

"You found nothing?"

Dan shook his head. "Not a damn thing. Might be that Jack was telling the straight. Them rocks *would* be a safe place to crap out for a while, happens you had enemies."

"You lunkhead, I've got more enemies than anyone in town, and do I crawl into the rocks like a stray dog?"

Fargo peeled a boiled egg, mulling his troubles. "Well, anything's possible, I reckon, but I don't credit Jack's words. Anyhow, this is Sunday. We got a little over three days to find out what the hell he's up to."

"Kill him," Dan said with stubborn insistence. "It ain't murder to shoot a rabid wolf."

"It might come to that," Fargo conceded. "There's women and even kids in this town."

Dan grinned. "Kids what murder their teachers."

Fargo, his back to a wall, saw Jimmy push through the batwings. The young marshal caught his eye and held his finger to his lips. Fargo saw the burlap sack in his left hand, and the shape within, and bit his lip to prevent himself from laughing.

"Well," Dan said, "we ain't doing so awful bad, Trailsman. You done killed three of the curly wolves in town, I killed one, and Jimmy has jugged four more. Happens we—"

"Look out, Dan!" Jimmy shouted from behind the old trapper.

A four-foot-long rattlesnake dropped into Dan's lap, and he loosed a shriek like a banshee, leaping up so fast that he tipped over his chair and would have fallen on his ass if Jimmy, laughing as hard as Fargo, hadn't caught him.

"Its head has been chopped off, you old fool," Fargo chided him as Jimmy went to toss the dead snake out the back door.

"I shot it down among the rocks," Jimmy explained when he returned. "Turnabout is fair play, Dan."

The old man's face was brick red, but he rolled with the punch. "I deserved that. Hell, I damn near pissed myself. I *like* to see a colt get his legs."

Tim Bowman, grinning like a butcher's dog, drew a beer and brought it to the new arrival. "It's on me, Marshal. That was a reg'lar floor show."

Fargo noticed the new layer of sunburn below the brim of Jimmy's high-crowned hat. "Nothing, eh?"

The merriment faded from Jimmy's features. "Not a blessed thing," he fretted. "What the dickens is Slade up to?"

"Hell, what's after what's next? People call him crazy, which he is, but forget that he's also smart as a steel trap."

"Hunh. I was just telling Fargo," Dan told Jimmy, "how the three of us is starting to make a little hay. But 'pears to this child like we're trapped twixt a sawmill and a shootout."

"You wanna spell that out?" Fargo said.

"D-e-d-d, dead—is that plain enough? Happens the red devils don't kill us, the white devils will. And Slade is the topkick of the devils."

"Any devil," Fargo replied, "can be sent packing back to hell."

"My stick floats the same way as Skye's," Jimmy declared, showing a new optimistic side. "I been running *my* traps, too, Dan. A few of the mine owners are in a stew because the small-claims men have banded together since the night that Fargo saved Bo Gramlich."

"Good to hear," Fargo said. "Damn good. But if the big bugs are in a stew, it's got to boil over."

"They won't just turn the other cheek," Jimmy agreed. "But between the nightly patrolling by you and Dan, and Bo's organization growing, some of the night riders have pointed their bridles toward the last productive mines in California. Some of Bo's bunch are even guarding my prisoners right now."

"Yessir, that news is rain to dry earth, Jimmy," Fargo said. "But we can't let up now."

"*You* sure's hell can't," Dan muttered. "Here comes the Cleopatra of the Comstock, and she ain't here to discuss the weather."

Smooth Bore reached the bottom of the stairs and flounced over to Fargo's table. "Morning, longshanks. Care to come upstairs and pet my puppy?"

"It's a fine puppy," Fargo assured her, "but I'm a bit under the weather today."

"I'm sorry to hear that."

Fargo was lying, but he suspected Tit Bit was lying in wait, and pleasing the two hungry sisters at once was a Herculean task a man couldn't take on too often—like staring directly into the sun, it could get dangerous.

Smooth Bore next glanced at Jimmy, whose boyish good looks and wide-as-a-yoke shoulders had caught her interest months ago.

"How about you, Marshal Helzer? Why don't you come upstairs and give me some . . . protection?"

Jimmy looked like a man staring down the barrel of a Sharps Big Fifty. "Ma'am, I . . . you see . . ."

Dan guffawed, Fargo grinned, and Jimmy—in deep and going deeper—just kept stumbling over his own tongue. Smooth

Bore bent close to his ear and whispered something. Even with his sunburn it was easy to see Jimmy turn scarlet.

"What'd she say?" Dan demanded the moment Smooth Bore left.

"You kidding? It would make a horse blush to repeat what she said."

"Hell, me 'n Fargo ain't horses," Dan pointed out. "What'd she say?"

Jimmy stubbornly shook his head. "I'm a Christian. I won't repeat it."

"Leave the lad alone," Fargo interceded. "That woman scares you, too, Dan. Besides, the show is starting."

For the next twenty minutes the three men enjoyed watching the talented troupe of acrobats, jugglers, and magicians who had made the Wicked Sisters saloon famous throughout the Far West for lively entertainment.

Again Fargo gazed intently at the performers, lost in speculation.

"What the hell, Trailsman?" Dan said to him. "You been hittin' the Chinee pipe?"

"Nah. Just thinking how there's more weapons than just guns and knives."

Dan's wild gray eyebrows touched in puzzlement. "Hell, a titty baby knows that. You got axes, hatchets, clubs—"

"Lock it up, Methuselah. It was just a manner of speaking."

"All I speak is American and cussing."

The early show ended and the three men started to rise from the table. Just then, however, a petite blonde in an organdy-trimmed dress and ribbon-laced slippers approached their table. Her black felt hat sprouted pansies.

"Do you remember me, Skye?" she greeted Fargo.

"Sure. Jenny, isn't it? You're one of the gals I saw when I first rode into town."

"Oh, you *saw* me, all right. All of me."

Fargo chuckled. "A very pleasant sight, too."

"Shove your feet under the table, sugar britches," Dan invited.

Jenny shook her head. "This ain't a social call. I'm in enough trouble just for talking to Skye. I best be quick."

"What is it?" Fargo asked the soiled dove.

"Last night I was . . . you know, with a Schofield hired gun name of Chilly Davis."

"Sure. We know who he is."

"He was drunk out of his gourd, so maybe it's all bunk. But he claims a bunch of night riders are going to bust them jailed regulators out sometime late tonight."

"I thank you, lass," Fargo said, giving her hand a squeeze. "Now dust, and be careful."

"I wouldn't kick *her* out of bed for eatin' crackers," Dan said, watching Jenny retreat.

"Jimmy," Fargo said after the pretty little whore had gone upstairs, "you know these mine guards pretty good. Would they get up a rescue team on their own steam?"

Jimmy mulled that. "With that bunch it's usually each man for himself and the devil take the hindmost. I'd say one of the toffs is behind it, and Septimus Dunwiddie is the wheelhorse driving most of the trouble. Looks like he wants to stop the loss of hired guns."

Fargo nodded. "Yep. And I think I'm gonna steal a march on him. There's another little matter I been meaning to . . . discuss with him."

The aptly named Enterprise Street was located where most wealthy areas of cities were usually found: above everyone else. The wide brick-paved thoroughfare was lined with neatly clipped hedges and imposing walls. Unlike the merely pleasant street Luce and Loretta Perkins lived on, this one boasted newly built, wealthy mansions—and private guards abounded.

Fargo turned in at the house Jimmy had described: a gaudy turreted monstrosity more expensive than tasteful. An armed guard stood before an iron gate. The sun had set an hour earlier, and the only light came from a lamp hanging on the gate.

The guard squinted, trying to identify the visitor. "Mister, you must be lost. Drifters dressed in buckskins don't—"

He paused. "Buckskins. Hell, you must be Skye Fargo—I mean, Mr. Skye Fargo?"

Fargo nodded. "I could do without the 'mister.' I don't say excuse me when I fart."

The guard laughed, instantly relaxing. "These rich whip-dicks *do* put on the airs, don't they?"

"Sing it, brother. Septimus sent word he wants to talk to me about working security for him."

The guard chuckled. "That's the boss for you. He musta heard that rumor about Ephraim Cole trying to hire you. Well, I'll guarandamntee, Fargo—the money's better here."

"We might be working together. What's your name?"

"Well, *this* summer it's Seth Carlson."

The guard pulled a metal locking pin from the gate and swung one of the sides inward. "Use the side door with the diamond window in it. Ned, his bodyguard, will answer. Don't make any sudden moves with him—he kills first and asks questions later."

Fargo had to ride at least thirty yards up a crushed-stone drive before he reached the side door. He reined in among shadows and swung down, hobbling the Ovaro. Pulling some rawhide strips and a bandanna from a saddle pocket, he approached the door and banged the brass clapper.

"Who is it?" a hardy, no-nonsense voice challenged after perhaps thirty seconds.

"It's me, Ned—Seth. I might have trouble out here."

The door swung open and Fargo, standing to one side, grabbed a fistful of the guard's greasy hair. Not giving a damn how much damage he did to the lackey, Fargo cracked his head hard against the jamb. The guard grunted once and then his bones seemed to melt as he collapsed at Fargo's feet, out cold.

Fargo quickly bound and gagged the man.

"Ned?" called a querulous voice from the interior of the house. "Who is that?"

Orienting toward the sound of Dunwiddie's voice, Fargo made a beeline through several sumptuously appointed rooms complete with textured walls and marble fireplaces. He found Septimus Dunwiddie in the main parlor reclining on a brocade divan with a snifter of brandy in one hand.

The speculator's face turned ashen. "You?"

"Yep. It's just me and you, muttonchops. Cozy little evening to home."

His hand trembling violently, Dunwiddie set the glass down on a stand beside him. Fargo noted he looked much less cocksure and commanding than he had in the Wicked Sisters.

"Where's Ned?"

"I'd say he's in cloud-cuckoo-land right now," Fargo replied. "But you're safe with me—*if* you keep your hands away from any hideout guns. Try a fox play with me and I'll send you over the mountains."

"Naturally you want money, Fargo, and you came to the right man."

Fargo was amazed to see that the man's snide smile was back. Fargo's assurance that he was safe had evidently restored his confidence.

"No," Fargo corrected him. "I want information. There's a raid planned for tonight against the jailhouse. And you're the puppet master, aren'cha?"

Dunwiddie, his hand steadier now, picked his drink back up. Turning his stiff cameo profile to Fargo, he swirled the amber brandy in its snifter, took a delicate sip and patted his lips with a pale blue handkerchief.

"I?" he finally replied. "Fargo, a lie travels halfway around the world while the truth is still putting on its boots. You've been woefully misinformed."

"The devil can quote Scripture for his purposes, Dunwiddie. I'm asking one more time, and if you're wise you'll stop skating around the edges—are you behind this raid?"

"Fargo, we are both powerful men within our chosen spheres. I know that illiterate ruffians such as yourself bristle at fancy quotes, but to cite a philosopher I admire: 'Whatever in creation exists without my knowledge exists without my consent.' Is that too abstract for your practical mind?"

"Christ, I'm getting goose bumps. And your consent is required if a man wants to go on living. Is that the point?"

Dunwiddie drank another mincing sip of brandy, his fleshy lips pursing. "Well, not for *you*, of course. You're a man's man. I mean the mudsill rabble who labor like Chinamen all their lives for hog and hominy and a filthy little hovel infested with rats."

Fargo moved closer in a few long strides, jerked Dunwiddie to his feet, and backhanded him hard and fast. Fargo didn't stop until the man's eyes were glazed and both split lips pouring blood.

"My God!" Dunwiddie pleaded. "Please! I'll call off the raid!"

"Like hell you will—I'll see that you don't. Your paid dirt workers are in for a surprise, and after tonight you'll be paying even higher wages to keep those sewer rats around."

Fargo roughly threw the perfumed barber's clerk back onto the divan. "I got one more question, and if you start playing ring-around-the-rosy with me, I'll knock your damn teeth out. What kind of squeeze are you putting on Luce Perkins? Now talk out."

Dunwiddie swiped a hand across his bloody mouth. "Luce Perkins . . . the head mining engineer at the Schofield? Why, we may have had a tiff . . ."

Fargo was at the end of his tether with this worthless speck on humanity's ass. More important—he had just clearly warned him what would happen if he sandbagged one more time. Fargo's iron-hard right leg flew up like a steam piston, the heel of his boot driving hard into Dunwiddie's mouth. Fargo heard front teeth crack when Dunwiddie's head slammed back hard. There were too many thick interior walls for the guard out front to hear his feminine shriek of pain.

Blue steel filled Fargo's fist quicker than eyesight. "Quit blubbering and lissenup, gal-boy. I got no use for any son of a bitch who threatens the life of a woman. What's the squeeze?"

Dunwiddie was past defiance—long past it. Blood fountained from his ravaged mouth, bits of broken tooth rinsing out with it, and the intense pain had him gasping and whimpering. "Fargo! Fargo, Christ Almighty, you've killed me!"

Fargo holstered his gun and snatched the Arkansas toothpick from his boot, holding the narrow ten-inch blade inches from Dunwiddie's left eye. "I swear to God I'll carve your eyeball out like an onion. *What* did you tell Luce Perkins?"

Dunwiddie curled into a ball, his breath rasping. He spoke with a lisp now. "Fargo, all the blood . . . Christ, you've killed me."

"Set it to music, you soft-handed maggot. Now talk out or I'll snuff your wick for good."

"I . . . I told Luce he has to greatly undervalue the veins under the Schofield mine so that Ephraim Cole will sell it to me. I . . . oh, *God* that hurts . . . I told him Nash Booth will kill his daughter if he doesn't."

"All that's over as of now, right?"

Dunwiddie nodded.

"And you know what happens to you if anything happens to Loretta *or* Luce?"

"God yes! Fargo, the pain . . ."

"Cut the sob stuff," Fargo snapped, pulling the remaining rawhide strips from his pocket. He bound Dunwiddie's ankles and wrists and gagged him with his own dainty handkerchief, the man screeching with pain when Fargo shoved it into his mouth.

"Be glad for it," Fargo told him. "It'll stanch the bleeding. And this way you won't call off your 'secret' raid. When we get done putting your bootlicks through the meat grinder tonight, they won't be too damn sweet on you, *Dim*widdie. Matter fact, to take a page outta your book—they might not give their consent for you to exist. You got some rough trash on your payroll, and they *will* perforate your liver."

As Carlson opened the front gate, he said, "What about it, Fargo? Did he hire you on?"

"I couldn't pass up the money, Seth. Say, the boss asked me to tell you—nobody comes inside for a few hours. He's got some tidy little blonde named Jenny in there with him, and they're playing hide the picket pin."

"Jenny? That little sparkling doxy from the Sisters? Christ, she'll eat that perfumed dandy alive."

"She will," Fargo agreed as he gigged the Ovaro onto Enterprise Street. "But, brother, what a way to go."

Just before midnight the seven men rendezvoused at the tiny jailhouse: Marshal Helzer, Fargo, Snake River Dan, and the prospectors Bo Gramlich, Paul Robeck, Billy Fredericks, and Lloyd Slaughter. The room bristled with weapons and there wasn't room to stretch.

"The hell's this all about?" one of the prisoners demanded, noticing all the rope Fargo and Dan carried in. "A hemp committee?"

"Did you get the lanterns, Jimmy?" Fargo asked, ignoring the question.

"One for each of us—fresh filled with coal oil."

Cromwell, the Yellow Jacket thug in the billed cap, yelled out, "Helzer, you bug-humper, we need more water back here."

"Drink your own piss, mouthpiece," Fargo told him. "If you

don't puke it up, you might last another day. Not that it matters."

Fargo suddenly brought his Henry's muzzle up to the ready, trained on Cromwell. "This is it, boys," he told his companions. "Let's kill these graveyard rats."

All seven men trained scatterguns, rifles, and handguns on the prisoners, whose arrogant expressions turned to whey-faced fear.

"Christ! A firing squad," Cromwell managed. "Muh-Marshal, you said we'd get a trial. Hell, this is flat-out murder!"

This was all bluff, Fargo's plan for scaring some of the vinegar out of these cocksure paid killers so they could be more easily bound and gagged. And it worked—in just a few minutes they had all four men trussed up on the floor. Now no warnings could be shouted to their companions.

"Let's head topside, Jimmy," Fargo said. "Fellows, bring your lanterns."

Jimmy had already propped a simple scaling ladder behind the jailhouse. Fargo waited until the other six had gained the flat roof, then handed his rifle up and carried the lanterns up in two trips.

"Well, Marshal," Fargo said as he took up a position, "run us through the plan."

In fact it was mostly Fargo's plan, but he realized that his take-charge manner—honed by necessity, not personality—could not be helping the young lawman's confidence.

"Not much to it," Jimmy said. "We turn the wicks on the lanterns as low as we can and light them. Then we set them at the back of the roof so the light won't show up front. After that we wait until our guests arrive and get close to the jailhouse. Before we even fire a shot, we toss the lanterns. Then we pour the lead to 'em."

"Wait for the marshal's signal before we do anything," Fargo added.

The seven men lighted and placed their lanterns, Paul Robeck staying with them as rear sentry. They settled in for a wait. The saloons and gambling houses were still rollicking, and night riders preferred to strike in the still of the night when others couldn't join in against them.

Bo Gramlich had taken up the position on Fargo's right. "Mr.

Fargo, I never did thank you proper for what you done—you know, stopping them regulators from taking my claim. *How* could I have been so hawg-stupid? Jesus, I saw everything except the three waltzing elephants."

Snake River Dan, on Fargo's left, chuckled. "That's what mining-town liquor does to a man, Bo. I watched some jasper in Cherry Creek set his own hair on fire after drinkin' forty rod."

"You've reformed yourself, Bo," Fargo said. "That's the main mile. Organizing the small prospectors is the last thing these mine owners and speculators like Dunwiddie want to see."

"That shines," Bo agreed. "At first, after you saved me from ruin, I still figured it was time to cut loose from these diggings while I was still above the horizon. But then, well . . ."

"But then you got mad, right?"

"Mad as a peeled rattlesnake," Bo admitted. "Figured I'd rather die with a spine than live without one."

"*That's* medicine," Dan approved. "Although Fargo would rather die with a hard pecker so he can screw the devil."

Another hour ticked past and Center Street began to close up for the night. Fargo, busy watching the street, noticed Jimmy nervously working his piece of hangman's rope. Fargo snatched it from him and flung it into the street.

"Now we're going to win this battle," Fargo promised him.

"*Now* is right," Dan said. "I think I see our lice crawling in from the west. Here's the fandango, boys!"

Fargo, too, spotted the shadow riders, holding their horses to a quiet walk from the direction of the mines. They had fanned out abreast in the wide street, and he counted a dozen. The moonlight was generous and before long he recognized Nash Booth riding a few paces ahead as leader. His lupine features looked granite-hard with determination.

"Steady, gents," he told the rest. "Keep your finger outside the trigger guard. Remember, it's not likely they know anybody's laying for them. So let's keep the element of surprise until Jimmy gives the order."

The jailhouse below them was dark and silent. The night riders rode in to within thirty yards.

"Helzer!" Booth shouted. "Send them prisoners out now or you'll soon be cold as a basement floor!"

A few of the prospectors anxiously watched Jimmy, wanting him to give the signal. But Fargo was surprised at the young man's admirable patience, and it paid off—the killers below followed Booth as he rode to within spitting distance from the roof.

Booth's short gun spat a streak of red fire and a window shattered.

Jimmy gave the high sign and the men ran back for the lanterns, turning the wicks up full before rushing forward and flinging them into the men with devastating results for the regulators. Burning coal oil smeared men and horses, panicking the mounts.

Fargo saw one thug take a direct hit to the chest and immediately explode in flames. His screams of abject pain rent the air even as his horse bolted through town, fanning the flames hotter and higher. Near the east end of town the bullets in the flaming thug's shell belt began cooking off like Chinese fireworks.

By now the men on the roof had opened up with a vengeance on their enemy. Scatterguns blasted buckshot, Dan's Dragoons roared like small cannons, and Fargo's Henry spat so much lead that, later, the wiping patch sizzled when he ran it through the bore.

Fargo searched for Booth before realizing he had been the first to escape. Before the rest of their thoroughly routed enemy could flee, however, some managed to toss a few hasty shots toward the exposed men on the roof. Jimmy gave a sharp grunt and went to one knee, holding his left forearm.

"Just clipped your wing, Jimmy!" Fargo called encouragement. "It's a long way from your heart!"

The entire fracas could not have lasted longer than two minutes. When the men climbed down they found four regulators in the street, two dead and two seriously burned and wounded. Without a word Fargo tossed finishing shots into the wounded. The fifth dead man was still burning in the street at the other end of town.

"The one down the street is Sam Watson," Bo said. "I recognized his horse."

"That's five more mercenaries killed," Fargo said as he tied off Jimmy's minor wound. "And others must be burned and wounded. I predict the garbage is going to scatter broadcast now. When it comes to stick or quit, these white-livered bastards quit every time."

"What about these rat droppings in the street?" Dan asked, toeing one of the corpses.

"Just leave 'em," Fargo said. "They'll serve as a reminder to the rest. And now the pigs can feast on their own."

11

Dr. Dale Lyons had a small walk-up office over the Gold Room saloon. Fargo's knock dragged him cursing from the leather-bound examination table where he slept.

"Don't you drunks ever use the other doctors?" he groused as he opened the door. "Christ, I haven't slept an hour straight—say! What happened, Marshal?"

The three men trooped inside. Lyons, a homely little man with rumpled clothing and kind eyes, carefully peeled back Jimmy's bloody shirtsleeve.

"I caught a bullet just now," Jimmy explained. "It hurts like the dickens, but there's not much blood now."

"You didn't *catch* a bullet, son. It whistled right through you. That's damn lucky. Thanks to these Indian raids I have no more liquid morphia for pain. And believe you me, if I had to cut a slug from that arm you'd have plenty of pain."

The doc glanced at Fargo, then Snake River Dan. "Just now, you say? That big shootout that woke me up? I thought the red-skins had finally laid siege to Virginia City. Hold still, boy. This has to be done."

From long experience with gunshot wounds, Fargo and Dan knew that Doc Lyons had to scrape the caked blood out until the wound was bleeding fresh to flush the dirty blood out.

"Say, Doc," Dan said while Lyons wrapped Jimmy's wound in gauze that had been soaked in gentian, "you got any medicine for rheumatiz?"

Lyons uttered a brief, rueful laugh. "Sorry. I have plenty of 'nostrums' that aren't worth a plugged peso, but very few effective medicines that are actually curatives. The two or three I have, such as quinine, I dare not dispense. The yahoos in this town don't understand the concept of 'doses.' They figure if they take all the medicine at once they'll be cured faster."

Dan looked startled. "Won't they be? That's what I do."

Lyons sighed at this cussed human ignorance. He handed the marshal an envelope. "There you go, Jimmy. Take one of these for the pain."

"But it says it's headache powder. I got no headache."

"Never mind that nonsense—that's just to keep the ladies feeling respectable. It's a generous dose of morphine. You'll sleep for a bit. Here's another for later."

"Better hold back on that second dose, Doc," Fargo said. "This lad will need a clear head for what's coming."

Doc Lyons eyed Fargo. "I'd say you're the healthiest specimen of manhood I've ever seen, mister. You have a clear conscience, don't you?"

Dan snorted. "Hell, Fargo don't know what a conscience is, Doc."

"Do you?" Lyons demanded.

"Happens I can't spell it, I ain't got one. Neither does Fargo."

"Oh, yes, he does," the medico gainsaid. "I can tell at a glance that this nation could use a lot more like him."

Dan waved this aside. "That's folderol. Would you trust your wife or daughter with him?"

"If you mean trust him to protect them with his life, yes. Absolutely."

Dan looked nettled. "Well . . . I reckon that much is true. But this randy—"

"Thanks, Doc," Fargo cut in, pressing two silver dollars into Lyons' hand. He respected frontier doctors, and liked this one, but all this discussion of himself as if he were a museum exhibit bothered him.

"Hunh," Dan grumbled as the trio cautiously descended the outside steps in the dull, leaden light of dawn. "*There's* a queer duck. Clear conscience, my lily-white ass. Hell's bells! Why, Fargo is guilty of brawling, womanizing, gambling, drinking, beating the shit out of crooked lawmen, evading arrest, and jailbreaking."

"The doc didn't say I couldn't have fun now and then," Fargo pointed out.

"Who *needs* a dang conscience, right Jimmy Boy? We killed five men tonight and we're *proud* of it, eh?"

"Not me," Jimmy said. "I almost puked when it was over. A believer can never be proud of killing even when it's necessary. It means something to take a man's life. If it don't, then none of us matters."

"Attaboy, Jimmy," Fargo approved.

"Everybody's a damn psalm-singer now," Dan grumped. "But can a man get a mother-lovin' pill for his rheumatiz? Hell no."

"Jimmy," Fargo suggested, ignoring the crusty trapper, "why don't the three of us bed down at the jailhouse? We can go turn-about on guard duty in two-hour shifts. That way each man gets four hours sleep and we'll be back on patrol before noon. You have to take that medicine, so I'll stand first watch while you and crab-ass sleep."

"He'd trust his wife with *Fargo*?" Dan muttered to himself. "That sawbones is a bigger fool than God made him . . ."

Fargo had a strong hunch that, after the bloodbath at the jailhouse, no regulators would be showing up any too soon. But he hadn't survived so long on the frontier by assuming the best. While Dan and Jimmy settled in to sleep, he pulled a chair out front and propped his Henry against it.

First, however, he had his two friends level their weapons on the prisoners while he untied their ropes and gags.

"Listen to me, Cromwell," Fargo said to the Yellow Jacket thug, "because I'm only saying it once. You're the high card in this deck of jokers. One peep out of *any* of you while we're trying to sleep, and I'll kick your teeth out the back of your head."

However, Fargo soon realized his warning was unnecessary. These men had heard the screaming and dying out front and knew damn well their peers had gotten the crappy end of the stick. They were also starting to realize that a prison stretch or even a gallows might be in their future.

"Can't we at least get some grub?" Cromwell grumped, chafing his wrists to restore circulation.

"The law says I owe you water and two meals a day," Jimmy said, "but it doesn't say what food I have to give you."

Jimmy handed him a canteen and a cheesecloth sack filled with cold, stale biscuits. Fargo stood first watch out front, noticing the street was unusually quiet. He rousted out Snake River

Dan at seven o'clock and slept the dreamless sleep of the bone-weary until Jimmy shook him awake at eleven.

"You got any popskull, Dan?" Fargo asked as he pulled on his boots.

"Jist some mescal in my flask."

"Trot it out, old son—if it won't deprive your horse."

"Hell and furies! Saint Fargo's having a morning bracer."

The liquor almost burned a hole in his empty stomach, but Fargo welcomed the slight perk to his somber mood.

"Got any spyglasses, Jimmy?" he asked. "Mine are back at the livery."

The youth pulled a pair from the top drawer of his desk. The trio went out into the dusty alley between the jailhouse and the adjacent dry goods store. Fargo led them about a hundred yards down the mountain slope, training the glasses on the Truckee River just to the north.

"That's godforsook country out there," Dan opined, shading his eyes from the desert glare.

"God may have forsaken it," Fargo replied, "but the red man sure hasn't."

"Wha'd'ya mean?" Jimmy demanded.

"Looks like the Paiute moccasin telegraph has got calls going out far and wide. I see mirror flashes being relayed way past the Humboldt River. And east into the Great Basin."

"Heap big doin's," Dan said.

Fargo nodded. "I'd say it's a gathering of the tribes—or of the warriors, anyhow."

"But you blew up all that stolen black powder, Skye," Jimmy said. "Wasn't *that* the secret weapon that gave them the guts to attack a large settlement?"

"That's a belief filtered through longing, not logic, Jimmy. I took out a threat that could have blown or burned down half this city. But once Sis-ki-dee gets his feathers in a ruffle, he can fire up entire red nations."

"Think they got enough warriors?" Dan asked.

"Well, that's got me treed. According to the latest scouting report I saw at Fort Churchill, Chief Yellow Bear's Bannock braves are five hundred strong. Medicine Flute has a Shoshone band in the Washoe Valley. It's smaller, but that bunch is suspected of having repeating rifles—as many as two hundred stolen army Spencers. There's no official report on the Paiutes, but I saw hundreds of wickiups."

Jimmy said, "Pete told me these far-west tribes know nothing about marksmanship. That they think magic guides the bullet."

"Yes and no," Fargo said. "Guns smoke, spit fire, and make noise, so they're magic. But redskins are dead shots with a bow and arrow, so they have some notion of aiming. They puzzle it out pretty quick. Hold it—"

Fargo focused the binoculars finer after spotting movement closer to Mount Davidson. He concentrated on a line of creosote bushes perhaps a half mile out. A patch of buffalo hair tied to a stick was raised above the bushes.

"Christ. They're trying to draw fire to probe our defenses. The attack *is* coming, stout lads. Indians are naturally lazy creatures, and they wouldn't go to all this trouble unless they intend to hit the warpath."

Jimmy heaved a resigned sigh. "How soon?"

"Happens they're still putting out the war call," Snake River Dan replied, "they ain't ready quite yet. And wunst they gather, they'll need to paint and dance. Indians won't attack until their medicine is right."

"Dan's right," Fargo said. "I'd say three days at the earliest."

Fargo cast a glance around. "It's too late to put up piked logs, and anyway there's not enough wood for it."

"Then we best sound the alarm," Jimmy said.

"Nix on that, Marshal—not this soon. If there's a panic, there's only one trail to Sacramento, and a rough one through mountains. The pilgrims will be picked off like lice from a blanket. The warning can't go out until it's too late to leave—that way they'll have to fight."

"There's a lot of men in this city," Jimmy said. "And a lot of firepower. I think we can beat back an attack."

"So do I," Fargo agreed. "That turkey shoot we had last night was just money for old rope. But if these three tribes grease for war, it won't matter if they're eventually driven back into the desert—they'll kill hundreds and wound that many more."

"There's no help for it now," Dan said. "It's fight or show yellow."

"I don't know about that," Fargo replied, mulling an idea that had been germinating in his mind for several days now. "Sometimes it's fight or show clever."

"That's too far north for me, Trailsman. The hell you mean?"

"You and Jimmy will be the first to know, old son. C'mon, boys. Let's go brew some coffee and pretend we live in peaceful times."

Fargo boiled a handful of coffee beans on the conical Sibley stove in the jailhouse while Dan kept an eye on Center Street from the open doorway.

"Here comes Bo Gramlich," Dan announced, "and happens he smiles any wider he'll rip his cheeks open."

"Mr. Fargo," the elated prospector said as he stepped inside, "it looks like that shooting affray last night has broomed the worst of the curs out of town. They're leaving in droves right now—headed back to California."

Fargo looked at Jimmy and Dan, barely suppressing a grin at the irony of their escape route. "Right now, you say?"

Bo nodded, not realizing the area was boiling with angry Indians. "Marshal, the Miners' Committee—working under your authority, of course—is strong enough now to take over security until you get those deputies you need."

"Bo, has Nash Booth skedaddled?"

"Not yet. Willard Jones and Sam Watson are both dead, but Chilly Davis is still siding Booth. They've deserted that old powder magazine, though. We can't locate them, but I suspect they're laying low at Dunwiddie's house."

"That's all damn good news," Fargo said. He glanced at the sullen prisoners. "But we best not tack up bunting just yet, boys. When it comes to killers in a boomtown, there's plenty and to spare."

"Dang, Skye," Jimmy said after Bo left, "you boiled this coffee too long—I just chipped a tooth on it."

"Strong coffee is a tonic on the frontier."

"Maybe so, but dyspepsia runs in my family."

"Then start thinking about going back east because a weak stomach can kill a man out here. I've been forced to boil my boots and belt down in starving times."

"Jimmy's right," Snake River Dan pitched in. "You're a good man, Fargo, but damn my eyes if your coffee don't taste like river bottom."

"Well, why don't you call the maid and order in some fresh?"

A kid of about sixteen, wearing the square red cap of a message runner, appeared in the doorway. "Mr. Fargo?"

"Yeah, kid. What you got?"

The lad entered the office and handed Fargo a chamois pouch. "It's from Mr. Luce Perkins at the Schofield."

Fargo tipped him four bits and opened the pouch, shaking the contents into his palm.

"Moses on the mountain!" Dan exclaimed at sight of the gold cartwheels. "Five double eagles! This child ain't glommed one hunnert dollars since God was a boy. You poke his pretty daughter and he *pays* you?"

Fargo read the brief note that tumbled out with the coins. "'Thank you, Fargo—Dunwiddie has apologized and claims he was only bluffing about hurting Loretta. Bluff or not, I'm convinced she is now safe thanks to you.'"

"Saint Fargo's at it again," Dan remarked. "Works miracles and such but his coffee tastes like burro piss."

The three men stepped out into the street.

"Speaking of Dunwiddie," Jimmy said, "look at Doc Panning's office."

He pointed toward an office with a giant gold-painted molar over the door. Fargo watched an obviously shaken Septimus Dunwiddie exit, supported by the bodyguard named Ned. Wads of bloody cotton protruded from the speculator's mouth.

Dan chuckled. "You musta messed his choppers up good."

"He'll never eat an apple again," Fargo said. "Killing a man is too lenient. But destroy his teeth and he'll suffer for life."

Fargo studied the wide street. "Looks like Bo was right. I don't see a regulator anywhere."

"'Cept for the one headed toward us right now," Dan said. "God's lieutenant."

Terrible Jack Slade, smiling affably, drew up in front of them. "Top of the morning, gents. Looks like you three have done a fine job. The curly wolves are running away like their asses are on fire."

This was the Jack Slade, Fargo realized, who people liked: tall, strong, handsome, and amiable. But he was deadly poison in a pretty bottle.

Fargo nodded. "'Preciate the kind words, Jack. Maybe now that the worst elements are leaving, you won't have to bring the Wrath down on the rest."

"What, *that* drunken nonsense?" Slade tossed back his head and laughed. "Say, that was all bluff and bluster caused by cheap whiskey. I've settled down now. I quit drinking, and I've even got my old job back as a silver engraver."

"Glad to hear it," Fargo said before Slade tipped his hat and moved on.

"You believe that malarkey?" Dan said.

"Sure, and I believe birds migrate to the moon."

The three men began walking again.

"So wha'd'we do about it?" Dan demanded. "It ain't but two days now till Wednesday. I say—"

"I'm the U.S. marshal," Jimmy interrupted him, "and I have to work this trail out for myself."

Snake River Dan harrumphed. "Sonny, you best leave this to—"

Fargo elbowed Dan hard, sending him a warning glance.

"Hell, you're right," Dan amended himself. "By God, you're the law, and this is your deal."

Five minutes later they had reached the slatted batwings of the Wicked Sisters. Jimmy finally spoke up.

"Skye, would you agree that whatever Slade's up to has to do somehow with those rocks near the Schofield?"

"I'd bet my horse on it."

"I'd bet Fargo's horse on it, too," Dan affirmed.

"All right. I say that, beginning at sunrise on Wednesday, at least two of us stake out those rocks."

"Good plan," Fargo agreed. "But don't forget that Indians prefer to attack out of a rising sun. This bunch is on us like a cat on a rat, and if they attack on Wednesday, we won't have time for Cannibal Jack."

12

Fargo had just left Paddy Welch's flophouse on Silver Street, bearing south on a cross street toward the Bluebush Café, when he felt a sharp tug at the folds of his buckskin shirt.

Less than an eyeblink after the bullet narrowly missed his lights, he heard the metallic crack of the rifle. All of an instant lead was pouring in at him, near-lethal slugs snapping past his ears. The gunfire was unrelenting, and Fargo was caught in the open. He detected at least two shooters, and from the volume of fire he concluded they had an arsenal of loaded weapons.

Realizing death was only a hairbreadth away if he did nothing, Fargo did the only thing that made sense—he lowered his head, charged headlong toward the nearest window, then leaped. He curled into a ball in midair and braced for impact, shattering glass and wooden frame as he literally broke into the building.

Fargo splashed into hot water, heard a woman gasp, then felt himself being washed out onto a linoleum floor in a deluge of soapy water. He looked up and saw a huge woman at least twice his age lying beside him, naked as a newborn. The washtub was still rolling.

"My stars and garters!" she sputtered. "What in the name of—"

"Ma'am," Fargo said as he drew to his feet in the sopping mess, "are you all right?"

"Right as the mail. Did those gunmen hit you?"

"No, thanks to your window."

More for his own sake than hers Fargo grabbed a rough cotton towel from a chair and flipped it over her. "Here's a five-dollar gold piece to cover the damage. My apologies for disturbing you."

"Don't apologize for saving your life. That was a smart move."

Fargo turned the heavy tub upright. "I *should* mop up that water, but I need to get a bead on those ambushers. Is there a back door?"

"In the kitchen. Good luck, young man. Thanks for brightening my day."

Fargo let himself out, then jacked a round into the Henry's chamber and moved cautiously along the side of the little clapboard house until he reached the street.

"Mr. Fargo!" shouted a young boy's excited voice. Fargo spotted the same red-capped messenger from yesterday. "Sir, it was Nash Booth and Chilly Davis who fired at you! I seen 'em!"

The kid pointed north toward the Truckee River. "I think they're still on the slope holing up in thick brush. Maybe a half mile down."

"Thanks, son. Would you like to earn an easy dollar?"

"I'll tell the world!"

Fargo flipped him a silver dollar. "First, get behind cover and *stay* there—no heroics. Then watch that slope until I get back with my horse."

Fargo sprinted to the livery on Center Street and tacked his mount. As he was leading the Ovaro out of the barn, Jimmy and Snake River Dan rode in. They had been searching that tumble of rocks and boulders near the Schofield mine.

"What's on the spit?" Dan greeted him. "We heard the gunfire and figured you for a gone beaver. Say . . . how come you're soakin' wet?"

"Had a little mishap. C'mon, boys. We got some quail to flush. Booth and Davis, to chew it fine."

The trio rode back to the cross street where the kid was standing vigilant guard behind a stack of wooden barrels. They tied off their horses and ducked behind the barrels.

"Did they move?" Fargo asked the messenger.

"No, sir. Now and then one of the horses moves and you can see its rump through the brush."

"Good work, lad. Now dust."

"Don't make sense," Dan said. "Why hole up in a spot like that?"

"Panic. They thought they'd kill me certain-sure. Now they're stuck and hope I don't know where. Seems likely they're waiting until nightfall so they can slip out of town with the rest that are making tracks. It wouldn't be a bad spot if the kid hadn't spotted them."

"There's just one problem," Jimmy said. "I doubt if they know that warpath Indians are hiding out there along the river."

Fargo grinned. "Yeah, that is a problem—for them."

He studied the terrain to the north. The green slope of the mountain gave way almost immediately to parched desert. Near the Truckee River was a swath of grass as high as the knuckles of a full-grown buffalo. It appeared peaceful enough, but Indians were experts at cover and concealment, and that grass was high enough to hide patient braves lying flat.

"Boys, you're looking at the meat that feeds the tiger," Fargo said. "We can charge them, all right, but they might not break in the direction we want them to. First we need to rattle them good. Check your loads."

"Those two men were soldiers," Jimmy said in a disgusted voice as he thumbed reloads into the cylinder of his pinfire revolver. "Deserters who were court-martialed. My brother Pete would cut off his right arm before he'd violate his oath. How can so many soldiers desert and become hired killers?"

Fargo and Dan, less naïve, exchanged a silent glance. Army life had never attracted the meek and clean, and Fargo had seen firsthand how the insane policy of enlistments as short as three months meant that most troops were green, poorly trained, and often criminals on the dodge from civilian star-packers.

It was Dan who answered the young man's question. "On account most men ain't honest like you and your brother, Jimmy. Take longshanks here—that lanky bastard would steal Tiny Tim's crutch, happens he could swap it for some quiff."

"Oh, I'd make sure he was sitting down when I took it," Fargo defended his ethics. "Now, here's the plan. We—"

His jaw dropped open in astonishment when Booth and Davis suddenly burst out from cover, hopping and dancing and slapping at themselves as if burning embers were lodged in their clothing.

"K.T. Christ!" Dan exclaimed. "Those nickel-chasing fools musta holed up in a spot packed with anthills."

"Red ants," Jimmy added. "Some an inch long. That slope is crawling with them."

Fargo grinned. "We won't get straight beads from here—we'd

need buffalo guns at this distance. We'll get horsed and rush them. Dan, hook wide on the left flank. Jimmy, do the same on the right. You two will be the pincers while I pressure the rest. Give 'em a lead bath. You can ride down to the desert floor, but don't venture very far out."

All three men hit leather and fanned out as Fargo ordered. The two killers below saw the charge and leaped onto their horses. At first they spurred their mounts left, perhaps hoping to hide in one of the mines. But Snake River Dan had closed some of the distance, and his intimidating Colt Dragoons forced them to scrap that plan. Escape on their right side was also pointless because Jimmy had "quartered the wind" on them and was also rapidly closing in.

Fargo kept it hot behind them with his Henry, the sixteen-shot magazine ideal for this kind of chase—as was the Ovaro's superior speed. His bullets were ranging in closer, but it was Nash Booth himself, when he reached the desert floor, who sealed his own fate. Like Lot's wife he had to take one last look back, and that was the split second Fargo needed.

The Henry kicked against his shoulder, and a big chunk of Booth's lower jaw was turned into bloody pulp. He almost fell from his saddle but recovered at the last moment and followed Davis out onto the glaring white sand. Clearly they hoped to gain the river. Fargo slacked his shots, knowing that overheating could scrape the bore badly and render the weapon permanently inaccurate.

By now the two desperate outlaws had pushed their mounts to an all-out run. Fargo joined his companions where they had reined in just beyond the base of Mount Davidson.

"You think the Paiutes are out there?" Jimmy asked him.

"Watch that line of creosote bushes on the left," Fargo replied. "Here comes the Wrath Slade's been batting his gums about."

Only moments after Fargo finished speaking he watched a Paiute sentry rise from behind the bushes and pull a finger across his forehead, signifying the brim of a hat: white men approaching.

"Buck up, Jimmy," he warned. "You ain't likely seen this before."

A minute later the two fleeing criminals reined in at the river, and Paiute braves literally swarmed on them. Even at this distance their terrified screams were clearly audible as their scalps were sliced in quick outline cuts and then wrenched from their heads. Both men were castrated and the bloody members shoved in their mouths. Halfway back up the mountain, Fargo looked back and saw both heads mounted on pikes.

"Well, Christian," Dan asked Jimmy, "I guess you don't approve of what you just seen, huh?"

"I'm an Old Testament Christian," he replied. "It put me off my feed a mite, but I'd say justice was done."

"*There's* a stout lad."

"We better all be stout," Fargo said, having glanced farther north. "Look."

A huge yellow-brown dust cloud swirled over the horizon.

"I'd say that's Bannocks coming to join the Paiutes," Fargo said.

"They say you're the best scout in the West," Jimmy said, "so I believe it. When you think the attack is coming?"

"Well, like Dan said, they got to powwow and dance and grease for battle. I'm thinking Thursday at the earliest, maybe Friday."

"Damn good thing we're up on a mountain," Dan said.

"High ground usually helps," Fargo agreed. "I once held off a bunch of Border Ruffians in Arkansas because I was on top a steep hill. But then again—if the battle turns against us here, where the hell we gonna go?"

Nash Booth and his three henchmen had once been the vile and evil heart of the regulator crowd in Virginia City. Now all four were dead as last Christmas. Riding through the streets of the city, Fargo spotted only a few "private deputies." Jimmy assured him they were no scrubbed angels but not likely among the killers and claim stealers.

"Skye," he said, "I know we talked this over already. But if an Indian attack could come as early as Thursday, it seems like we need to warn the citizens and prepare defenses, doesn't it?"

"I'm wondering about that. 'Citizens' in a town like this are usually just a mob in an emergency. You got any siege weapons?"

"Pete sent us a two-pound howitzer and copper slugs to load in it. Since the eastern slope of Mount Davidson is the easiest, we can put it there."

Fargo nodded. "Yeah, we'll put that in place. But I've never met a tribe yet that's stupid enough to stand in front of field guns, and the Paiutes and Bannocks use excellent tactics. Does the city have a warning system?"

"Steam whistles at the mines."

"All right, that's warning enough. There's enough weapons in this town to arm the city of London. If these hotheads and drunks are warned too early, a bunch of them will get drunk for days and have a redskin party. They'll end up killing each other and doing stupid things that get themselves killed. That's what happened at Pyramid Lake."

"Fargo's right," Dan tossed in. "The liquor around here would make a rabbit attack a bulldog."

"I can't deny any of it," Jimmy agreed. "But I worry about not having a first line of defense."

"I b'lieve we'll have one," Fargo said.

"What?" Jimmy and Snake River Dan demanded at once.

"I been talking to Smooth Bore and Tit Bit about that. We're still working it out."

Dan howled with derisive mirth. "What, you gonna stop war-path savages with frilly dainties?"

"Leave it alone," Fargo snapped. "If I talk out, it could get all over town. Besides, we may be in worse trouble with Jack Slade. You two found *nothing* in those rocks this morning?"

"Ain't a *damn* thing among them rocks," Dan insisted, "'less you count the puddle of piss I left there."

"I dunno, Skye," Jimmy said. "I just don't see how anything coulda been overlooked. Heck, I practically got every stone, rock, and boulder named and memorized. Could be he just went down there to throw us off the real trail."

"He's wily enough to do that," Fargo admitted. "But don't forget how he just appeared out of thin air. I still think there's a tunnel or something he disappears into."

"Hey!" Jimmy said, pointing upslope to the top tier of houses. "Smoke. It looks like Dunwiddie's house on Enterprise Street."

The three men hit the next cross street and gigged their mounts up the slope. The bucket brigade had done a good job of tamping down the flames, but the front of the house was mostly smoking embers.

Fargo led his friends through the side door he had used the

first time he was here. They found Dunwiddie in the rear parlor, shot full of holes.

"The place has been sacked," Fargo said, glancing around. "Even the paintings off the walls. Prob'ly his own people did it when they lit a shuck out of town."

"Lookit there," Dan said, pointing at the dead man's open mouth. "Doc Panning drilled in some dog teeth for him after Fargo kicked out his real ones. Fat lotta good it did him. Think Dunwiddie had a *conscience*, boys?"

"He ain't got one now," Fargo pointed out.

Jimmy gave an audible sigh. "You fellows can joke, and he sure deserved to die. But this is yet another murder, and until I get some permanent help I can't investigate any of them."

"You can call it murder, law dog," Dan replied. "Somebody killed the bastard graveyard dead, and *this* child is all for it."

"You two cracker-barrel philosophers need to quit grazing so wide," Fargo advised. "Jack Slade watch starts tomorrow at sunup, and those Paiutes and Bannocks will likely be dancing into a trance pretty soon. That's why I'm going to see Smooth Bore and Tit Bit again right now."

Snake River Dan looked flabbergasted. "You're getting your wick dipped while Virginia City burns? You horny toad."

"No," Fargo said as they headed outside through the acrid smoke. "But I will be gambling. One roll of the dice, and if I lose we're all gonna be in one world of hurt. So you'd best wish me luck."

13

After Fargo woke up, a half hour before sunrise on Wednesday morning, he lay still for a few minutes just listening. The habit had saved his life more than once.

Instead of the dawn chorus of birds or the soughing of wind in the trees, however, all he heard was the sawing racket of snoring men and the creaking of weak joists in Paddy Welch's big frame flophouse. The Trailsman longed to put Virginia City behind him and return to the dangerous but pristine wilderness, the only place he truly considered home.

He shook Snake River Dan awake and both men pulled on their boots in silence, allowing the hardworking men around them to enjoy sleep a few minutes longer. Jimmy met them in front of the Bluebush and they went inside for breakfast.

"This ain't bad grub," Dan allowed as he poured sorghum over a stack of cold buckwheat cakes. "But this child ain't had no Cincinnati chicken in many moons."

"What's Cincinnati chicken?" Jimmy asked.

"Bacon," Fargo replied, finishing up his coffee. "There's lots of slaughterhouses in that city."

"Plenty of pigs running around this town, Dan," Jimmy pointed out.

Dan scowled at the kid. "And they ain't exactly corn fed, neither."

"I take your drift. I wondered why nobody was butchering them out."

"All right," Fargo said. "Everybody's got his marching orders. Me and Jimmy take Jack Slade vigil down in the rocks at the base of the mountain. Dan, Jimmy has lined up Bo Gramlich and other volunteers from the Miners' Committee to help on Indian watch. We need an experienced hand in charge of them, so you'll stay up here as topkick."

"Experienced hand," he grumped. "This shit's for the birds. You only call me that when you're tryin' to get me killed."

"Hell, you're an old geezer too ornery to die on your own—*some*body's got to send you to the rendering plant, hoss."

Dan chuckled. "Fargo, I'd whip the shit outta you but then your buckskins would be laying on the ground empty."

The trio went outside onto Center Street just as the sun cleared the eastern horizon in a roseate flush. The day already felt hot and a dry wind blowing from the Mojave Desert to the south make it hard to even spit.

Dan went to join the volunteers on the northern and eastern slopes of Mount Davidson while Fargo and the young marshal recruited their horses and headed down the western slope.

"Maybe we shoulda just walked," Jimmy said. "Now we have to hide our horses."

Fargo nodded. "Yeah. But my prediction about when the tribes might attack could be off by a day or so either way. Indians are experts at confusing and surprising their enemies. This heap big medicine man Sis-ki-dee is a Contrary Warrior. That bunch are known for violating the law-ways. They might skip rituals like putting on war paint and praying to their gods."

"Yeah, I got it. Who wants to run a mile uphill if savages attack?"

"For now," Fargo said, "it's Terrible Jack Slade we need to worry about. If my gut hunch is right, he means to somehow destroy Virginia City."

Fargo glanced carefully around before tugging rein and veering off into the well-sheltered willow copse where Loretta Perkins and her father sometimes met for tea and reading sessions. Both horses had tanked up good at the livery. Fargo decided on short tethers instead of hobbles since their mounts might be there quite a few hours.

They approached the clutch of rocks and boulders from opposite sides, hands filled with blue steel. First they searched every nook and cranny to make sure he wasn't already hiding.

"Seems clear," Jimmy said.

"Yeah, aboveground."

"You still think he's going down under the rocks?"

Fargo nodded. "I do. Where or how, I don't know. Let's hole up and watch for him. This big granite boulder gives us a good view in all directions."

"Man, it's already hot," Jimmy complained. "Say, what's that?"

Earlier, Fargo had pulled a rawhide drawstring bag from a saddle pocket. Now he opened it and pulled out two of the strangest objects Jimmy had ever seen.

"It's sponge-and-leather footgear," Fargo explained, pulling them over his boots. "Designed them myself for army contract scouting. They're quiet and they barely leave a track. Once, a Cheyenne Dog Soldier started to kill me, then saw these and ran away."

Several hours passed, the granite boulder heating up and forcing the two sentries to positions in the shade. The clamorous sounds of drilling and blasting, the shrill steam whistles of the skips arriving and departing, jangled on Fargo's nerves.

The two men shared some beef jerky and warm water. Jimmy mopped at his brow with a red bandanna. "You know, Skye, this all-day watch was my big idea. But do you think maybe Jack was telling the truth when we saw him on Monday—that maybe he *has* reformed?"

"Terrible Jack Slade will reform when all the oceans turn to lemonade. You had a good plan and I say we stick to it. Somehow, some way, these rocks are the keys to the mint."

Two more hours passed, and the sun was westering. Fargo felt bored and sleepy, but a long habit of vigilance kept his mind from wandering. He estimated, from the slant of the shadows, that only about eight hours remained until midnight—the hour when Slade promised to unleash forces from hell on Virginia City.

"Still awake, Marshal?" he said in a low voice to Jimmy, who was out of sight about fifteen feet away.

"Yeah, but my eyelids keep drooping on me."

"This is the time to stay sharp, star man. He could—"

Fargo suddenly shut up, blood throbbing in his temples. "Stay out of sight," he called to Jimmy. "Slade just turned off the freight road and he's headed this way."

"Yeah, I see him."

"We don't make a sound or move," Fargo added, "until he reveals whatever it is we've been looking for. If you hear me challenge him, stay hidden in case he pulls a fox play."

Slade appeared to stroll casually toward the tumble of rocks and boulders, but his face showed suspicion and nervousness. Fargo tried to press even tighter into the space between two boulders, hoping the waning sunlight would help to conceal him.

Terrible Jack made a quick pass around the pile, hands on the butts of his fancy Remingtons, then headed right toward the center of the pile. Fargo rose to his knees, shuddering inwardly at sight of the necklace of shriveled human ears around Slade's neck. The big man stooped over a slab of gray shale that appeared embedded in the ground.

With a mighty grunt he lifted the slab and flung it aside.

"Freeze right there, Jack," Fargo called out in a voice that brooked no defiance. "Don't even twitch unless I tell you to. You're under the gun, and if you buck me just once it's curtains for you."

Slade obeyed but his eyes were mutinous. Both men watched each other at daggers drawn. Fargo stepped into full view in the mellow golden light.

Slade brought out his charming smile. "Sure, Skye. I got nothing to hide."

"Mm. Now listen. Grab those shooters between your thumbs and forefingers and lift them from the holsters *slow*, then drop them. Use more than the fingers I said, I'll powder-burn you."

"Sure, sure. See, I done just like you ordered. But I *ain't* gonna drop them on these rocks. Look at the grips, Skye—that's mother-of-pearl inlay. Cost me a hundred dollars in Saint Louis. Can't I just lay them down? How in the hell can I shoot you when they're dangling straight down from two fingers?"

The question was logical and Fargo saw his own short gun as a valuable tool.

"Set 'em down," he relented, "but you're covered by a second man in the rocks."

Slade laid both six-shooters carefully down. "Thanks, Skye. That's mighty white of you. Those shooting irons are my pride and joy."

"Keep your hands out from your sides," Fargo ordered. "We'll need to check you for hideout guns. Jimmy, c'mon out."

"I got a Brasher over-and-under derringer in my right boot," Slade admitted, "and a knife in my left boot, but it's just a little one for cutting whores and such."

Jimmy was still climbing out of his awkward position between two small boulders when Slade made his surprise move. Undetected by Fargo, he had palmed a rock when he laid his pistols down. With snake-swift speed he hurled it at Fargo's head at close range.

Fargo's catlike reflexes helped him get his right arm across his face in time to block the throw, but the sharp rock cracked hard into his elbow, instantly numbing the arm and making it fall to his side, temporarily paralyzed and useless.

Fargo had no time to transfer the Colt to his left hand because Slade was hurtling straight at him, knife in hand. Reacting from muscle memory, not thought, Fargo tried a trick he had learned from mountain-man lore: the swinging snapshot, used when the trappers were too weak from hunger to lift their heavy Hawken guns.

Fargo spun around fast in a circle, momentum lifting his arm, and got off one shot. It hit Slade just under his left collar bone but didn't stop him. Fargo sidestepped the knife and switched the Colt to his left hand, but by then he was seriously off balance on the uneven rocks and about to trip as Slade, snarling like an enraged wolf, closed for the kill.

Fargo went down, shots rang out, and he heard bullets splat against the rocks. In a heartbeat Slade's left eye was replaced by a thick rope of blood, and Terrible Jack folded like an empty sack, dead from a brain shot.

"You okay, Skye?" Jimmy asked in an anxious voice.

"Yeah, thanks to you, Marshal. I *knew* you were up to fighting fettle. You saved my life. That damn rock hit my crazy bone, but it's wearing off now."

"Dang, I got myself wedged in those rocks. Is he . . . ?"

"Dead as a shucked oyster," Fargo affirmed. "C'mon. Let's see what's under the shale slab."

"I never thought to pull that up," Jimmy lamented as he belted his gun. "I just figured it was embedded in the ground."

"Don't kick yourself. Me and Dan missed it too."

Enough light remained for Fargo to duck his head through the opening and see five or six feet inside. "Why, it's a big underground room. And Slade has a lamp within reach. Let's see what he was up to."

Both men dropped inside and Fargo thumb-scratched a lucifer to life, lifting the chimney off the lamp to light the wick. As the flame rose higher it pushed the shadows back and revealed a large dugout.

"What the heck is it?" Jimmy asked, perplexed.

"You mean what was it," Fargo corrected him. "I'd bet a dollar to a doughnut it was a temporary fort for a party of mountain men back in the days of Bent's Fort. If this was a colder climate I'd call it a winter fort. That rusted metal by your foot is the iron stake from an old beaver trap. I'd guess they were headed for the Sierra, likely coming due west from the Wasatch Range, when the local tribes started to worry them."

Fargo stepped in farther, raising the lamp. "Look at the back wall. You can still see the sally port they made for quick escapes. It's blocked now by rocks, but that was before all this blast rubble was hauled over here from the Schofield."

"Well, it's interesting history and all," Jimmy said, disappointment keen in his voice, "but how could this place be a threat to Virginia City?"

"Jimmy, I'm damned if I'll hot-jaw any man who just saved my life. But a lawman has to take a close look before he declares a trail closed. Let's check the walls starting right behind us. You go to your left, I'll take the right. I'll set the lamp in the middle of the chamber, so rely on your hands."

Both men had been poking and probing for about twenty minutes when Fargo encountered a mound of loose dirt at the base of the north wall. He grabbed the lamp and called Jimmy over to help him scoop the dirt away, revealing an opening large enough for a man to easily crawl through.

A cool breeze tickled their faces. Fargo poked the lamp through. "It's another opening—a good-size tunnel you can walk upright in."

Both men crawled through and stood up, noticing the tunnel had solid rock walls.

"Heck, I recognize those blast scars," Jimmy said. "This is a drift—a side tunnel bored off a main chamber. Most likely the Schofield blasted it to mine gold ore under Mount Davidson, prob'ly before Virginia City was built on the slopes."

"That rings right," Fargo said. "They found a vein and followed it. It's a lot cooler down here than on the surface."

The upward-sloping tunnel was smooth and spacious. Water seeped through numerous fissures, explaining the moss-carpeted stones here and there.

Fargo, who had developed a good sense of time and distance over the years, felt a grim certitude when he guessed they were under the city limits. A few minutes later his conviction was borne out when the outer fringe of lamplight revealed a sight that made his skin crawl.

"Good God a-gorry," Jimmy almost whispered.

The discovery rocked both men back on their heels. Scraps of wood had been used to build a platform—a platform loaded with kegs of blasting powder, scores of sticks of dynamite, and even six-pound artillery shells used in the U.S. Army's muzzle-loading Parrot guns.

"That moonstruck bastard *did* plan to wipe out Virginia City," Fargo said. "And he would have, too—or at least a good chunk of it."

"The city is mostly wood," Jimmy added, "and the fires alone might have taken all of it."

Fargo said, "I don't see any timer mechanism unless we find it on his body. So he must've planned to go up in the explosion."

"Is this close enough to the surface?" Jimmy wondered.

"Lad, the solid rock gave way fifty yards back. Listen close."

Jimmy did, his face showing astonishment. "I hear a hurdy-gurdy, and only the Wicked Sisters has one. We're right under the saloon!"

"The way you say. And at midnight there'll be a couple hundred people there. All right, Jimmy, I'm staying here to guard this stuff. Go round up a bunch of your volunteers so we can haul it out. And whatever you do, don't pick any clumsy men."

14

With the old powder magazine where Nash Booth and his minions once stayed now deserted, Jimmy had the newly discovered explosives and munitions stored there. Using his federal emergency power of temporary confiscation, he declared the building city property and placed a round-the-clock guard on it from the Miners' Committee.

"So what's the plan?" Snake River Dan demanded when the three men met for a tasteless boiled-beef supper at the Bluebush. "Use the shit you found in that tunnel agin the savages?"

"It would scare them," Fargo conceded. "You saw how they acted when I blew up that black powder at their camp. But, Dan, you know Indians as well as any man. Like I said, they aren't stupid enough to stand still and get blown up. They don't use massed charges like white soldiers, either. They scatter without orders and rely on individual courage and initiative. But *dogs* will always attack in packs."

Jimmy looked startled. "You still think they'll hit us with wild dogs?"

"Fargo ain't just putting out air pudding, colt," Dan said. "This child has *seen* them curs. Way over a hunnert, I'd reckon, and half starved. That makes them meaner 'n Satan with a sunburn."

"They won't be the main attack, Jimmy," Fargo said. "Just a diversion to get us white skins all flummoxed before the braves strike in force."

"You fellows have fought more Indians than I've even seen," Jimmy said, "so I believe you. Well, the north and south slopes are long and steep with ridges dogs would have trouble climbing. So I guess it's the west or east slopes. Both have roads."

"Not likely the west slope," Fargo pointed out. "These are

half-wild dogs that have never seen piles of ore tailings, mucking buckets, giant steam drills, and all the other strange sights where there's big mining operations going on. It would scare the fight out of them and they'd scatter."

"Yeah, but they've never seen a town, neither, and that's where the east slope leads," Jimmy pointed out.

"True, but the mines are at the bottom of the west slope. They'll have to actually crest the east slope to see Virginia City, and by then the smell of white men will have them in a kill frenzy."

"And don't forget, turd," Dan told Jimmy, "these curs has seen lodges and wickiups. That's sorta like small buildings."

Jimmy shook his head. "Man alive, I got a lot to learn and dang little time to learn it."

"*This* man is alive," Fargo reminded him, "because of you and your steady nerves. Son, by planting Slade you saved countless lives today. Since you're a Christian, I say you'll earn jewels in paradise for what you did."

"Damn straight," Dan chimed in. "When I call you turd, I mean you're my favorite turd."

"All right, bottle it," Fargo snapped. "So we'll hit the dogs on the slope with black powder, dynamite, and Jimmy's howitzer. Copper slugs should shred them to trap bait. It won't stop the main attack though."

"It was quiet as a pharaoh's tomb out there today," Dan said. "Nobody spotted one featherhead. That's bad cess, Fargo. They'll likely hit us at sunup."

"Or even tonight," Fargo agreed, "though I doubt it. We're moving into half-moon phase, and they need light in a place brand-new to them. I still advise Jimmy to skip any general alarm unless all else fails. You've got ninety men in the Miners' Committee?"

Jimmy nodded. "They're already in place above the east slope."

"All right. Pick about a dozen more men you trust to stay sober and put them on roving sentry on the other slopes just in case. Remember, boys, it doesn't matter that there's enough men in this town to beat back an attack. Nobody holds a blood grudge longer than a warring tribe. For every brave killed, his entire clan swears revenge. If we want Virginia City to have a future, we need to convince these Paiutes and Bannocks that white-skin medicine is more powerful than Sis-ki-dee's."

"Hell, that's all spoke straight arrow," Dan said. "But ain't none of us a shaman. What's this damn mystery plan you got close to your vest?"

Fargo pushed his plate away and cracked his knuckles. "Just hush down and listen up. Here's the way we play this deal . . ."

While Jimmy was busy rounding up roving sentries, and Snake River Dan was grabbing a few hours sleep before returning to the slope, Fargo strolled down to the Wicked Sisters. It was ten p.m. and he found Smooth Bore conferring at the bar with Tim Bowman.

"Is everything set?" he asked the saloon owner.

"More or less," she replied. "Needless to say, they're not happy as larks. But they trust you—especially the women," she added with a wink. "Still, I had to offer a whopping bonus. It's a hell of a dent in our savings, Skye."

"Don't worry," Fargo said, quaffing half the beer Tim set before him. "I just talked to Jimmy. Every dollar you shell out will be replaced from the civic fund."

Smooth Bore brightened. "Jimmy I trust. Say, why don't you send him upstairs to see me sometime? That young man is well knit."

"Yeah, but he'll come 'unraveled' quick if you get hold of him," Fargo quipped.

Tim snorted, and Smooth Bore slanted a reproving glance at him. He moved down the bar a discreet distance.

"I shouldn't tell you this, long-tall," she said to Fargo, "but since I have to set up the faro rig anyway . . . do you know who Jenny is?"

Fargo nodded. "Sure. One of the gals in your stable. She warned me about the raid on the jailhouse."

"She's not just one of my gals—she's the prima ballerina. The girl is only twenty and she should be onstage in New York. I tried to talk her out of working here, but she wants money. And it costs a man ten dollars to enjoy her favors—*and* they have to bathe first. Anyhow, not one man in this town turns her head except you. She's been pining after you since the first day you came to town."

"Pining how?" Fargo said in a cautious voice.

"Don't worry, Skye. She's no mail-order bride. She wants the same thing me and Tit Bit want."

Fargo looked relieved. "She's a pretty little thing," he conceded. "And she's worth the money, I reckon. But as for the bathing first . . . I've spent enough time in bathtubs lately," he added, recalling both Loretta Perkins and the woman whose window he crashed through.

"Don't be a goose," Smooth Bore chided. "She wouldn't take a penny from you, and she'd do it with you in a buffalo wallow. She's not in love with you, Skye. She's in *lust* with you. I wish you'd give it to her good, really scratch her where she itches. Other men bore her, and I don't need a sporting gal who forgets to tell every customer, 'Baby, you're the best.' Put some zeal back in her work."

Fargo's lips pulled into a grin. "Well, if it's a matter of duty . . . which room is hers?"

"Number seven, right of the landing. And don't hand me that 'duty' malarkey, you horny bastard. You'd screw a snake if somebody held its mouth open."

"That's a stretch," Fargo said, and they both laughed at his pun.

In fact, Jenny had been on Fargo's mind ever since he spotted the petite blonde with the corn-silk bush running naked on the first day he entered Virginia City. Many soiled doves were homely as mud fences, but like Smooth Bore and Tit Bit she was a true beauty.

He ascended the stairs and rapped on the door of room seven.

"If you haven't bathed today," a lilting voice called through the door, "I'm not receiving company."

"I haven't bathed, Jenny," Fargo confessed. "But it's honest sweat."

The door opened almost immediately, revealing Jenny in a sheer silk chemise that clearly outlined her strawberry nipples. Her pale blond hair hung loose and unrestrained to her bare shoulders, framing a creamy-lotion face with wing-shaped green eyes and heart-shaped lips.

"Skye Fargo," she said, tugging him inside before closing and locking the door. "All I can think about is you riding me hard while I wrap my legs around you."

"Then let's get thrashing," Fargo said, instantly aroused.

She gazed at the tent in his buckskin trousers. "My, you're certainly ready. I'm flattered."

"Oh, I've *been* ready. I've thought about plenty since the first day I saw you in your altogether."

"You have?" she said, blooming. "I used to hate that disgusting running of the whores. But if it made you notice me, I'm glad for it."

She flicked him a cross-shoulder glance as she wiggled out of her chemise. Fargo draped his gun and shell belt over the footboard of the bed, then sat on a chair to tug off his boots.

She stood naked now, her skin flawless and glowing. He watched her discreetly splash a few drops of lavender water on her hard, pointy, high-riding breasts—breasts with ruddy areoles that ended in those beautiful strawberry nipples. Her butt, too, was firm and high, tight as a summer apple, and the legs flowing down from it were supple and well formed with perfectly turned ankles.

She crossed close to him and took his right hand, tucking several of his fingers up into her hot love nest. "Feel how ready I am? And we haven't even started yet."

Fargo worked at his belt with his left hand while his right cosseted her sex, making her gasp and grab hold of his shoulder as her legs went weak as India rubber. She tugged his buckskins down and stared with awe at his throbbing manhood.

"My glory! I thought Smooth Bore and Tit Bit were exaggerating. You *are* a stallion!"

Fargo stood up, swept her off her feet, and dropped her on the bed, settling into the saddle formed by her silky-satin thighs. He spread the soft folds over her nether portal and guided his iron-hard member into her, both of them groaning in abandon at the wave of hot pleasure tingling through them.

Fargo drove deep into her slippery and tight sheath, increasing the tempo as his own release grew imminent. Thank God, he thought, she was not a "talker" like Smooth Bore and her sister. Like him, she concentrated on the pleasure—and on getting all of it. He cupped his hands under her mother-of-pearl ass and lifted it off the mattress; she, in turn, locked her ankles behind his back, seeking all of his length.

She climaxed quietly but powerfully, shuddering hard each

time her passion exploded in release. Fargo delayed as long as he could then spent himself inside her, requiring many hard, concluding thrusts to finish.

For uncounted minutes they lay in a daze, limbs intertwined.

"Skye Fargo," her weak voice finally broke the silence. "Would I be greedy if I asked for seconds?"

"I hate to leave the table hungry myself," he replied, his manhood already stirring like a snake coming awake.

Just then, however, heavy gunfire erupted from the direction of the east slope of Mount Davidson.

"I guess we both go hungry," Fargo told her, swinging his legs out of the bed and reaching for his boots.

15

Sudden eruptions of gunfire, in Virginia City, were so common they hardly drew notice. Fargo, holding his Henry at a high port, hurried down the middle of Center Street, expecting to hear more shots and the piercing cries of attacking braves.

Instead, he heard only the usual raucous sounds produced by scores of saloons, brothels, and gambling houses. He found Snake River Dan just past the edge of town, still fuming.

"The hell happened?" Fargo demanded.

"Ah, them damn green-antlered fools," Dan replied. "One of Jimmy's roving sentries got spooked by a rooting hog and opened fire. A dozen more piss-brained idjits cut loose afore I got 'em to lower their hammers."

"No great harm done," Fargo calmed him. "That's bound to happen with trouble on the spit—especially after dark with green-horns. Remember that scrape on the Jornada in New Mexico Territory?"

Dan chortled. "*Do* I? Me 'n' you threw in with that bunch of teamsters when Apaches was salting their tails. Around midnight old Moss Hubbard cut a big old fart and them bullwhackers busted caps fir a whole two minutes, some of 'em crying out to their Maker how they didn't wanna have their dander lifted."

"And Apaches don't even scalp," Fargo added, both men laughing anew.

"Them was the shining times," Dan said nostalgically. After a pause he returned to the wake-a-day world and his voice grew more serious. "Ain't much to report. Jimmy's got the rovers in motion on the other slopes. The howitzer's been dragged into place over yonder on the little grassy bench just above the road. 'Pears to me most men in town ain't even twigged the game yet. Bo Gramlich's got these men disciplined good."

"What about the stuff me and Jimmy found in the drift?"

"Jimmy got that squared away. Fellow name o' Ron Bodine loaded it into a buckboard, covered with a tarp, and fetched it up from the powder magazine. It's under guard. Wouldn't take but two minutes to get it here. Say . . ."

"Say what, Methuselah?"

"What the hell *you* been up to? Ain't that lilac water this hoss smells on you?"

"Hell, I could be killed anytime. Naturally I'd want to taste a little frippet one last time."

"Fargo, I swear to Crockett you'd screw a knothole in a fence."

"I'd plane it for splinters first and glue some fur around it. Even *I* got standards."

Dan laughed so hard that one of his Colt Dragoons almost popped out of his sash. But in his usual fashion, his mood turned instantly surly and serious.

"Goddamn gut-eating heathens," he swore bitterly as he stared toward the dimly lit desert below them. "Ain't even safe for me to return to my cave in the Sierra. Hell, I had coyote, lynx, and wolf skins drying on the stretchers—won't be able to soften the hides now. War is all these western tribes care about, Skye. Why, they ain't even harnessed the wheel or writ down their own lingos in thousands of years."

"You're tossing a wide loop, old son. The Cherokees had newspapers before most whites did, and the Navajo silversmiths got reg'lar contracts with jewelry shops on the Ladies' Mile in Manhattan. But my stick floats the same way as yours on this war-fever business. I believe in live and let live, but too many red men are like the white slaveholders in the South: they don't see that freedom is every man's natural right."

"Ahuh, that rings right," Dan agreed. "This bunch about to attack us got no real grudge. This ugly old moth-eaten mountain don't mean pee doodles to them. It's only on account white skins are here—now it's holy ground."

"Never mind all that," Fargo said. "Things are the way they are, causes be damned. It's past midnight now, and I predict those dogs will be set on us at very first light—five hours from now or even less. Keep your powder dry and your nose to the wind."

"Ahuh, and what if this soft-brained plan of yours don't work?"

"In that case," Fargo replied, "just look at it as a free hair-cut."

As the night advanced and Orion brightened in the sky, Fargo decided it was time to bring in the best advance scout he knew—the Ovaro. The stallion was especially sensitive to the smell of bear grease, which many tribes used in their hair.

While a cool night wind fanned him pleasantly, Fargo rode in a circle around the crown of Mount Davidson. Now and then he called out to the sentries, knowing they were on the ragged edge and suffering from jangled nerves—and fully capable of filling his hide with lead in a tense moment.

Fargo was riding behind a cluster of dark buildings on the north side of town when the Ovaro abruptly snorted and pricked his ears forward. The Trailsman tugged rein, speared his brass-framed Henry from its saddle scabbard, and lit down on the near side of his horse, standing behind the Ovaro's shoulder. The moment he worked the lever with a loud metallic *snick*, he heard rustling sounds in the brush below him—Indian braves escaping.

Fargo resisted the impulse to open fire. Not only was it a waste of lead in the darkness, but a volley of fire now would send every man out there into a frenzy of useless gunfire.

Besides, from experience Fargo had a strong hunch he knew what the braves were up to. Leading his stallion by the bridle reins, he knelt and felt along the bottom of the closest building. In no time he found the first fire bundle—a bunch of highly flammable dried sage grass tied with animal sinew. A flaming arrow alone usually went out before igniting wood, but when enough were aimed at fire bundles, an entire settlement could be set ablaze in short order.

Fargo rode to the eastern slope and found Snake River Dan running a whetstone over the blade of his bowie knife.

"They've slipped through our net," Fargo said, showing the old trapper the fire bundle. "Get some volunteers to check all the buildings on the lower slopes. Make sure they gather these up."

"Shit, piss, and corruption," Dan swore. "I figgered we had these red sons locked out. Hell, mayhap the whole damn mountain is swarmin' with johns."

"Don't get your bowels in an uproar," Fargo calmed him.

147

"They only send a few of their best sneaks in to plant bundles. Just get the bundles gathered up. Where's Jimmy?"

"Working with the rovers and keepin' 'em frosty. That kid's some pumpkins when a scrape is coming. Damn it all, Fargo, I hate this waiting. It works on a man's thoughts."

"Yeah, the braves know that, too. You've heard the owl hoots?"

"Hell, I ain't deaf, boy. 'Course I hear 'em. Ain't no damn owls on this mountain."

"Won't be long now," Fargo said, noticing how false dawn glowed in the desert to the east. "I expect those yellow curs to come charging soon. You best tell Ron Bodine to bring that buckboard farther out of town. And send word to Jimmy to man the howitzer. I'll go tell Smooth Bore it's almost time."

Despite a stirring of belly flies, Fargo felt his blood singing. Not a trouble-seeking man by nature, he welcomed a good dustup that couldn't be avoided. Besides, with any luck this massacre now on the verge of being unleashed on both sides could be hog-tied by wit and wile.

He found Smooth Bore playing draw poker with Tim Bowman and skinning him alive.

"All right lady," he called over the batwings. "Time to post the pony."

Fargo returned to the slope. Bodine sat with one foot up on the brake to hold the buckboard in place on the incline. A helper had unloaded the kegs of blasting powder and drilled detonation cords through the bungholes.

"Boys," Fargo suggested, "it might be a smart idea not to use up all the powder and dynamite too quick on the dogs. Jimmy will be shredding them with copper slugs, and that might make them reverse their dust in a puffin' hurry. I'm hoping we can stop the red arabs in their tracks down on the flat. But if that plan goes bust, we'll need this stuff."

"That's what Marshal Helzer and Snake River Dan said, too," Bodine replied. "You just hum the tune, Mr. Fargo, and we'll dance to it. I ain't no leader, but I'm a damn good follower."

"It was damn good followers who spanked John Bull's ass and took this country from England," Fargo replied. "Good luck, gents. Every one of you is a credit to his dam."

The eastern sky showed a faint blush of the new day. Fargo

could not yet make out the Paiutes, Bannocks, and perhaps Sho-shones waiting down below, but they were there, all right. Des-ert warriors could dig quick sand wallows and scuttle into them like scorpions.

Jimmy showed up, hobbled his mount, and took up a posi-tion behind the howitzer.

"Skye, I can load the powder bundles, aim, and work the lanyard. But I'll need an ammo loader."

"I've loaded howitzers before with shells and grape shot, but how do I work these loose slugs?"

Jimmy pointed to a large keg filled with one-inch slugs, ser-rated to tear and rip. "See that metal scoop with the long beak on it? It holds two pounds if you don't overflow it. I'll tip the barrel up while you pour a load in. Then I lower it so you can jam in some cotton wadding and drive it home hard with the ramrod."

"You got yourself a loader, Marshal." There was just enough light to see Fargo's raffish grin. "But don't jerk that lanyard until my handsome face is clear of the muzzle. You'll break every female heart in the West."

Snake River Dan strolled up in time to hear this. "H'ar now! Them hearts won't break 'less he blows your pizzle off."

"Here comes the wild dogs!" shouted a sentry on the ridge just above them. "I can't make out the Injuns, but God-in-whirl-winds! Those curs look like a yellow wave rolling at us!"

"Every man Jack hold your fire until you hear the howitzer!" Fargo roared out. "You'll just be wasting lead if you open fire too soon!"

Jimmy tilted the gun's short barrel up and Fargo loaded and rammed the slugs. The snarling and barking grew louder as the killer curs reached the bottom of the slope.

"Bodine!" Jimmy snapped out. "They're fanning out in a wider line than we figured. Pass some dynamite out."

"Get a powder keg ready to roll down the slope," Fargo added.

The light was less grainy now and Fargo got a frightening view of a solid wall of maddened canines, fangs bared and dripping—far more than he and Dan had estimated.

"You're the gunner, Jimmy. Let her rip when you're ready."

Jimmy tugged the lanyard and the powder load detonated with an ear-ringing concussion, the gun recoiling back several feet on its carriage. Jimmy aimed well, and at least a half dozen lead dogs exploded into bloody gobbets of flesh and organs. Now the individual riflemen began a steady volley, but the dogs were small, moving targets and the gunfire less effective.

Several more times the howitzer belched its lethal load of slugs, and soon the slope was strewn with decimated dogs. Dynamite exploded at other points along the slope, hurling mangled corpses into the air.

"Light that keg and roll it," Fargo told Bodine, for despite the carnage some of the attacking animals were about to crest the slope.

The twenty-second fuse and the well-graded freight road combined for perfect targeting as a huge roar of smoke and fire snapped the back of the attack and flung dogs into the sky like confetti in the wind. The surviving animals, cowed and crying, scattered back into the desert in every direction.

"H'ar now, Fargo!" Snake River Dan exalted. "You said there ain't no buzzards in these parts, chucklehead. This child wagers they'll be here quicker 'n an Injin going to crap."

But Dan, still flush from victory, hadn't yet peered beyond the smoke still hazing the air. Fargo had, using binoculars, and a ball of ice replaced his stomach at the daunting sight below in the desert: mounted Indian warriors sitting their ponies in full battle regalia, so many of them that the line seemed to stretch to the horizon and beyond.

The buzzards would indeed feast, but more than dogs might be on the menu.

16

"Jesus H. Christ on a crutch," Dan intoned in a somber voice. "This hoss never figgered there *was* that many red sons."

Fargo and Jimmy were both using spyglasses to study the formidable array. Fargo recognized the hundreds of Paiute braves instantly by their plumed-hide helmets similar to those some Apache clans wore. The Bannocks, a fierce tribe even larger in number, were recognizable by their streamered lances and their ponies' roached manes. The Shoshone warriors, forming the northern end of the enfilade line, wore distinctive fawn-skin moccasins with intricate beadwork.

"Are they about to attack?" Jimmy asked, his voice tight with nervousness.

"Not yet," Fargo said. "When they show in force like that, and hold in place, it usually means the clan battle chiefs are bickering among themselves about what exactly to do."

"It was us makin' mincemeat of them dogs, Jimmy," Dan added. "Your big-talking gun and the dynamite and powder put some white in their livers. That's big medicine—heap bad medicine."

"Dan's struck a lode," Fargo agreed. "But we got one big problem, and his name is Sis-ki-dee. See that ugly, panther-scarred son of a bitch with the copper brassards on his arms?"

"The one riding up and down the line shouting at the others? Is he a chief?"

"Worse—he's the top Paiute shaman. Usually a battle chief rules the roost in war. But Sis-ki-dee is a Contrary Warrior, a crazy-by-thunder madman and a rebel against the old law-ways, and Dame Rumor has it that he killed the peace chief picked by the council of elders. Now he's got the battle chief and clan leaders spitting when he says hawk."

"And he's sayin' hawk to 'em right now," Dan opined after glancing through Fargo's binoculars. "He sure's hell ain't discussing the causes of the wind. Could you pop him over at this range, Fargo?"

"It would take a 750-grain bullet. Besides, we don't dare buck him out—you know that. He's a shaman, and that would curse the tribe if white skins killed him and they didn't settle the score."

"I reckon that's so. It's just, he's so cussed ugly I want him dead."

"Why are so many of those braves missing fingers?" Jimmy asked.

Snake River Dan snorted. "You didn't learn 'b' from a bull's foot back there in May Bee, Iowa, didja sprout? That's to show how much they miss a dead squaw or child. 'Course, it's never a trigger finger."

"Hey, Marshal Helzer!" a nervous voice called from the defense line. "That's a shitload of redskins down there! Ain't it time to sound the general alarm? If those red devils rush us, we ain't got the men nor guns to turn the charge."

Jimmy looked at Fargo with entreating eyes.

"James, you're the law, and it's your call," Fargo said. "But I say nix on that. You get all the drunk hotheads and Indian haters up here, and they *will* open the ball just for sport. Then the tribes will have to attack. Smooth Bore's got her people right behind us in the livery. Let's apply a little mentality—I say it will work."

"I hitch up with Fargo," Dan said, surprising the Trailsman. "Mebbe he spends too much time combing pussy hair out of his teeth, but no white man knows Injins better than the Trailsman does."

"Hold off, Lemuel!" Jimmy called back to the man. "They're a fair distance out, and there's still time."

This elicited some grumbling among the men, and Fargo feared they wouldn't stay disciplined for long if those braves broke into war whoops and advanced.

"Jimmy," he said, "if that jasper Lemuel or anybody else tries to set himself up as the topkick, kill him, you hear me? Just walk up and powder-burn him. There's too much at stake here. That's summary justice and it's legal under your emergency declaration."

Jimmy nodded. "I already had that in mind."

Fargo turned to Snake River Dan and spoke quietly. "Dan, pick thirty volunteers for an advance guard to go down with us. That's how many sticks of dynamite are left, and each man will have one hidden out of sight. They can wear sidearms, but tell them to ground their long guns. These tribes don't like the sight of them."

"Ahuh, volunteers . . . you been visiting the peyote soldiers? I know where this trail is headed, and you *won't* get no damn volunteers. This bunch ain't Rogers' Rangers."

Fargo nodded. "You're right, old salt. How 'bout it, Jimmy? Can we sweeten the pot?"

"We have to, I spoze. All right, Dan—each volunteer gets one hundred dollars in gold. The mine owners will cover it or I'll revoke their permits."

Jimmy and Fargo raised their binoculars again.

"Skye, I know what those hailstone patterns on their horses mean—they're out for a battle. But what's that tied on their wrists—medicine bags?"

"No, those are rawhide-wrapped rocks for close-in killing. These desert tribes don't have contact with many traders, so they don't have many war axes or hatchets with iron blades. But a rock will kill you just as dead."

Jimmy lowered his voice. "Skye, what if your plan don't work and they attack? What tactics will they use?"

That was a poser and Fargo had no certain answers. The usual pattern, when Indians attacked a forted-up position, was for the defenders to shoot clockwise while the Indians circled counter-clockwise. But this sprawling city on a mountain slope eliminated that tactic for both sides.

"Jimmy, it's a poor sort of an answer, but if we fail to stop them down on the flat, we'll just have to sound the general alarm and try to kill enough to ruin their fighting fettle. Red men don't lack for courage, but it's not their way to fight to the last man. Death, to them, is a taboo that brings misfortune to the survivors. One thing worries me, though."

There was enough light now to see that the weather was rare for this area: a cool, overcast day pregnant with the threat of rain.

"This weather," he continued. "Their bowstrings are made of animal tendon, and rain loosens them. They know that damn well,

153

and Sis-ki-dee might goad them into attacking fast before it rains. Pass the word—snap the arrows so they can't be used again. Usually a big group like this commences to yipping and chanting to nerve up, giving a warning."

Snake River Dan returned, quietly chortling. "That gold done 'er, boys. I got thirty volunteers. They're comin' now. But the word must be out how there's trouble—men are streaming from the saloons."

Suddenly a lone rider below broke from the line and rushed toward the mountain.

"Hold your fire!" Fargo roared out. "It's a trick! That's a buckskin suit stuffed with grass and tied to the pony. It's to lure fire and spot our positions."

Fargo glanced behind him down Center Street and loosed a string of curses. "Jimmy, turn that howitzer and fire over their heads. Stop them come hell or high water or we're in for a bloodbath."

Fargo realized that time was up and events had taken command. He shucked out his Colt and fired three rapid shots—the prearranged signal for Smooth Bore to unleash her unique army.

"Advance guard, follow me!" Fargo roared, and the fight to save Virginia City had begun.

17

It was a sight that transfixed every man watching, red or white. Fargo led the advance guard, followed by two drummers, a banjo player, and an accordionist, all belting out "The Yellow Rose of Texas." These tribes were unfamiliar with white men's music and instruments, and the strangely pleasing, yet slightly unnerving sounds froze them in place like mounted statues.

"Well, kick me in the nuts and call me Squeaky," Snake River Dan muttered. "They ain't moved an inch."

"Yeah, even with rain clouds making up," Fargo said, watching the sky darken.

The guard assumed wide intervals and the musicians moved to one side so the jugglers could be clearly seen. There were three of them, dressed in tights, bright red tunics, and red belled caps. Indians considered red the color of valor, and Fargo had instructed the soiled doves to make these new outfits.

Two men and a woman juggled bright red balls with amazing dexterity and speed, so many the braves were dazzled and astonished.

"Glom that," Dan said. "Mostly a warrior's face is like a slab of stone when he faces an enemy. This bunch is downright ex-fluxuated."

"Don't gloat," Fargo advised. "Sis-ki-dee's not so impressed. He ain't about to let this spectacle make him look puny."

"That egg-sucking varmint can eat shit and go naked," Dan snarled. "He needs to be sent over the mountains. I got a Kentucky pill for what's ailing him."

"Just hold your powder, hoss, until we know which way the wind sets. Revenge is a dish best served cold."

The eight acrobats came next, taking advantage of the natural slope to tumble rapidly down, then leap off one another's shoulders high into the air as the jugglers released brightly colored, gas-filled balloons that rose over the Indian warriors like a flock of colored birds, forcing many to gape in astonishment at this wondrous magic.

"Here it comes," Fargo said as Sis-ki-dee, riding an all-black pony with a flat buffalo-hide saddle, started tearing up and down the line, haranguing his warriors to attack.

"That red arab's got a pinecone lodged up his sitter," one of the guards remarked in a tense voice. "Maybe we *should* let daylight through him."

"Stow the chin-wag," Fargo warned the guard. "All of you just make sure your phosphors stay dry if it starts raining. If I give the order to light your dynamite, and it's raining, just drop to one knee and use your hats to cover the match. The fuses will burn unless it starts pouring. Throw it as far as you can into the featherheads and then pull foot back up the slope, but stay between the troupe and the braves."

Fargo was proud of the entertainers from the Wicked Sisters. Many had never seen a wild Indian, and all were scared spitless, but they had many lives to save and toward this end they bent all their efforts. Still, Fargo was worried—Sis-ki-dee appeared to be shaming some braves into more warlike faces.

"Here comes Merlin," one of the guards on Fargo's right said even as the wind picked up and Fargo felt a raindrop on his neck. Merlin was actually Drew Doty, Smooth Bore's cousin and the star performer at the Wicked Sisters.

This was the last card the white defenders had left to play, and it was literally a "hole" card. Merlin, an imposing figure in a topper and black cape with red satin facings, strolled boldly out to within fifty yards of the line of warriors. An arrow could easily have skewered him at any moment.

"*Parlay-vous francais*?" he roared out. "*Guten morgen! Mens sana in corpore sano! Soy un hijo del diablo!* Fuck all y'all and abra-goddamn-cadabra!"

Despite the tension of the moment, Fargo had to grin at this bravado. It all sounded impressively mystic and held the warriors spellbound.

"How many lingos was that?" Dan demanded. "I only caught the cussin'."

156

"I think I counted five with the English," Fargo said, "and one was Spanish, another French. But don't ask me to put names to the rest."

Merlin made several flowing motions with his cape and then tossed something on the ground in front of him. A huge puff of thick black smoke rose like an enveloping curtain. When the wind dissipated it, the man had simply disappeared.

This had a ripple effect on the warriors, who had closed in from both ends to see better. Exclamations broke out, and some braves even cheered the powerful magic.

But the show wasn't over. The female juggler ran forward, opened a big scarlet cloth, and when she whipped it away, Merlin was back, this time holding a black cat by the scruff of its neck.

Pandemonium broke out among the warriors, and Sis-ki-dee was apoplectic with rage, knowing this was mere trickery. Fargo had accomplished his goal—it now appeared to the assembled tribes that paleface magic was greater than Sis-ki-dee's.

"Why, hell's bells!" Dan exclaimed. "I saw Merlin climb out of a hole."

"Of course, pudding head," Fargo chided. "Jimmy slipped down and dug it last night. And the cat was in a cage. Do you think magic is real?"

"Why, you think I'm fresh off Ma's milk?" Dan replied, unable to disguise the disappointment in his tone.

Sis-ki-dee rode out in front of the warriors and pointed at Merlin, shaking a fist and exhorting the braves to attack. The brave magician defiantly stood his ground.

"He's got a set on him," Dan approved.

"Yeah, but I don't like this," Fargo said. "The warriors are pure-dee impressed by what they saw, but that bastard Sis-ki-dee has the evil road and slick palaver. If he shames their manhood enough, we'll be up to the hubs in redskins."

"Ain't he got more tricks?" Dan asked.

"Nothing to top that last one. Lissenup!" Fargo called to the advance guard even as thunder shook the ground. "Set your heels and nerve up! It might be coming down to the nut-cuttin'. If I give the holler, don't bother throwing lead—just dynamite."

However, there was one last, magnificent trick—and nature

played it. The thunderclap was followed, seconds later, by brilliant tines of lightning that ran along the ground in dazzling blue-white balls that raced along the surface until striking Sis-ki-dee and his mount. Horse and rider fell dead to the ground.

For uncounted seconds, red men and white were rooted, speechless and gaping. Merlin, however, had enough presence of mind to spread his cape and bow, claiming credit for the bizarre incident.

There was no panic among the warriors, and no one issued a command. As one, they raised their buffalo-hide shields in tribute to this great white shaman. Then, again without a command, they turned their ponies and retreated from the field of battle.

"Maybe so, better not," Fargo muttered.

Snake River Dan broke his shocked silence. "By grab, I'll be et fir a tater! Did you *see* that, Fargo?"

"You think I was asleep?"

"Well, mister, bloody business was close at hand. You *still* say there ain't no magic?"

In fact, Fargo had once witnessed "blue-ball lightning" during a terrible storm in the Sangre de Cristo Mountains of New Mexico. But now he gazed into the dark and sagging sky while the wind lashed refreshing tendrils of rain into his face. By now half the population of Virginia City had gathered on the slope above, and a raucous cheer broke out. Several of the advance guard had Merlin on their shoulders.

"No, Dan," he replied in a tone of quiet wonder. "I don't b'lieve I'll ever say that again."

"Ephraim Cole made good on every bonus himself," Jimmy reported on the day following "Merlin's miracle" as the newspaper broadsheets were already calling it. "And he's so happy about Dunwiddie being dead that he's paying the salaries for five deputies of my choosing."

"Yeah, he buttonholed me this morning," Fargo said as he tossed the blanket and pad on the Ovaro's back. "Offered me three hundred dollars a month to supervise security for the Schofield."

Snake River Dan and Jimmy exchanged a quick glance in the dim light of the livery.

"Three hun—? Skye, are you tetched?" Jimmy blurted out.

Dan chuckled at Jimmy's uncharacteristic outburst. "Pups will bark like full-growed dogs, I reckon. And he's right, Trailsman. That's a year's wages for most jaspers."

"You know gold ain't worth an old underwear button to me," Fargo said while he centered his saddle. "After being holed up here nine days, my needle's pointed toward the Sweetwater Valley. I like to go there to flush out my headpiece."

"Fargo, you've had jackrabbits in your socks ever since I knowed you," Dan said. "And a feller can't hardly blame you. Wunst a man tastes the waters of Manitou, the old legends say, it will always call him back. Called me back a few times when I was spry enough for the trip. But I reckon I've waltzed myself tired."

Fargo aimed a fond glance at his grizzled old friend. Both men knew, without having to say it, that given Dan's age they would never meet again. "Spry, huh? Hoss, you're tough as boar bristles and got the endurance of a doorknob. A man couldn't have a better man in a scrape. I'm mighty proud to know you, and the name of Snake River Dan is famous in the West."

Fargo was not one to lavish praise, and his remark took Dan by surprise.

The old trapper harrumphed impatiently. "H'ar now. A frontier man don't slop over like some weak sister. Goddamn gnat in my eye," he added, and Fargo pretended not to notice the moisture filming Dan's rheumy old eyes.

To cover his embarrassing moment, Dan quickly changed the subject. "Death by lightning was too quick for that rat bastard Siski-dee. Some of them fingernails he wore on his leggings come from children. He needed to be buried up to his neck in them anthills on the north slope and honey poured over his head."

"Lightning was too quick," Fargo agreed. "He never felt it. But it was dramatic as all hell, and that's why I wager the area tribes won't attack Virginia City again. They'll charge into the teeth of guns but not superior magic."

"Sure," Jimmy said, "but they'll likely keep attacking teamsters and express riders and the like, won't they?" he asked.

"You want egg in your beer?" Fargo teased. "That's why they're called *wild* Indians."

"Well, it'd sure be mighty fine to have you around a while longer," Jimmy pressed. "Dan's decided he's staying in Virginia

City. Tim needs help at the Wicked Sisters, so Dan's gonna be the back-bar man and swamper. Three hots and a cot and his drinks for free."

Fargo grinned. "That include mescal for his horse?"

Dan looked embarrassed at becoming a board-walking townie. "Never you mind, pussy hound. *This* child will still be singing the strong-heart songs."

This news about Dan was no news at all to Fargo. He had secretly made the arrangement with Smooth Bore and Tit Bit. Dan was over sixty now, and Fargo was damned if he was letting a man who saved his life die alone in a cave. Fargo knew the sisters would take good care of him.

"So won't you maybe change your mind, Skye?" Jimmy cajoled. "The three of us make a good team, don't we?"

In his mind's eye Fargo pictured the majestic mountains surrounding the Sweetwater Valley, with their magnificent basalt turrets and white-water creeks funneling into the draws, twisting and rioting southward. He couldn't put it into words, but he missed listening to the crackle of insects, the bubbling chuckle of the Sweetwater River, the soft song of the high-country winds. And after a stint in this lifeless desert country, he missed the wild iris painting the meadows and slopes, one of the prettiest sights in the American West.

"We were a fine team, Marshal *James* Helzer," Fargo replied. "But I belong out beyond the settlements. You just cover your ampersand, hear? Don't get cocky just because you'll have five new star-packers siding you—that ain't no army."

"No, sir, I won't forget."

"Always keep six beans in the wheel and remember—victory doesn't go to the fastest man but to the one who scores the first hit. Plenty of men have beat me on the draw, but they're worm fodder now."

"Don't you worry—I been taught by the best. Two of the best," Jimmy added, looking at Dan.

"You remember Dan's here, son, and he's survived everything from the Runaway Scrape in Texas to the Comanche Wars. You'll find good sap in old wood."

Fargo led the Ovaro outside and forked leather. "Well," he told his two friends, tossing them a salute, "I'm off like a dirty shirt."

Fargo cast one last glance around this bustling city built on a gold-rich mountain and then gigged the Ovaro into motion. With luck he would survive his long journey and rest for a while in the Sweetwater, and that was all he needed to know for now. As always, destiny would soon overtake him, giving him a purpose and a place to be.

LOOKING FORWARD!
The following is the opening
section of the next novel in the exciting
Trailsman series from Signet:

TRAILSMAN #355
TEXAS GUNRUNNERS

*Texas, 1860—where the Trailsman is about to learn
that no matter how bad things seem, they can still go south.*

Skye Fargo's lake blue eyes narrowed as the lone rider approached the little train of six wagons the Trailsman was leading from Galveston to San Antonio. Fargo hadn't expected to have a pleasant journey from Galveston to San Antonio, but so far things had worked out much better than he'd thought they would. He didn't want trouble now.

He'd been hired by Louis Charboneau, a New Orleans merchant, to see to it that Charboneau's daughter Michelle arrived safely in San Antonio, where Charboneau had opened a new mercantile store. Charboneau had hired a man to watch Michelle on the ship from New Orleans, and Fargo was to take over the job in Galveston.

Thanks to her father's description, Fargo had been prepared for a prim and standoffish young woman who cared nothing for the company of men. He had planned to endure the trip as best he could, since Charboneau was paying well, but he'd received a surprise when Michelle turned out to have quite an interest in him. A personal interest, you could say. Very personal.

Charboneau had been in touch with an immigrant group needing a guide, and he'd gotten Fargo that job, too. Being with the immigrants would give his daughter some extra protection, and Fargo didn't object. It would also give him more money.

Up until now, it was one of the easiest trips Fargo had ever made. No Indian attacks. No rain to churn up the Texas mud that could slow a wagon down to the pace of a rattler with a broken spine. Not that Fargo would have minded slowing down, since Michelle made his nights very entertaining. So entertaining, in fact, that Fargo almost regretted reaching San Antonio.

But the lone rider bothered Fargo. There was something furtive about the way he held himself and the way he glanced over his shoulder now and then. Fargo decided it would be a good idea to go out ahead to meet him, but first he had a word with Otto Schneider in the lead wagon.

"I don't like that fella's looks," Fargo said. "You be ready for trouble, and warn the others."

Otto was a short, wide man, solid as a butcher's block as he sat on the wagon seat. He was the kind of man Fargo would have liked to have along on any trip he ever made.

"I will do it," Otto said. "Fredrick!" A boy's head popped up behind him. "Jump out of the wagon and go down the line. Tell everyone that there might be trouble."

Fredrick didn't say a word. He slithered to the back of the wagon and dropped off. Fargo nodded to Otto and headed out on his big Ovaro stallion to meet the rider.

The man leaned forward in the saddle as Fargo approached, as if resting himself on his mount's neck.

"I'm hurt," he said, in a voice that was little more than a croak. "Need help bad."

The reins slipped from the man's hand, and Fargo knew he was expected to take them and lead the horse back to the wagons. He wasn't going to do that, however, until he was sure the man was really injured.

They were on a section of the rutted wagon road that was lined with oak trees draped with gray Spanish moss. The trees were so old that their heavy lower limbs touched the ground. Along with the thick brush that grew among the trees, there was plenty of cover for any friends of the man on the horse.

The man moaned as if begging for Fargo's attention, but Fargo kept his eyes on the trees. He'd heard of similar tricks being played on wagon trains on the way to San Antonio.

Looking off to the right, he detected a slight movement among the thick oaks and saw a brief flash of color that might have been a man's shirt.

Fargo wheeled the Ovaro around and headed back to the wagons.

The man on the horse rose up suddenly with a pistol in his hand. He fired three shots as men on horseback burst from the trees. All of them headed for the wagons, firing their guns as they rode.

The Ovaro threw up clods from its hoofs as Fargo passed the first three wagons. All of them had come to a halt, and Fargo could hear the cocking of rifles.

He pulled back on the Ovaro's reins and stopped the big stallion at the third wagon, the one where Michelle no longer sat on the wagon seat but lay in the wagon bed. Thanks to Fredrick's warning, she'd been ready to take cover when the shooting started.

The riders had reached the wagons by that time, but the immigrants were ready for them. Rifle fire came from all the vehicles. Fargo pulled his big Henry from its sheath on the Ovaro and jumped into the wagon. He looked back at Michelle, who grinned at him. The girl had spunk. Fargo returned the grin and fired off a couple of shots at the riders, all of whom had concealed their faces with bandannas.

A bullet ripped through the wagon's canvas cover. Michelle said, "Who are those men, Skye?"

"Bandits. They were looking for easy pickings, but they got a little surprise."

Fargo fired the Henry again. His shot hit one of the riders, who fell forward onto his horse's neck, dropping the reins. Another rider did what Fargo hadn't done and grabbed the reins. He turned aside, pulling the wounded man's horse along with him.

The rest of the would-be robbers took this as a signal that

they weren't going to get what they'd been looking for, and they all swerved away from the wagons. In seconds they had vanished in the trees.

"Are you all right?" Fargo asked Michelle.

"I am just fine. How could I not be while being guarded by Skye Fargo?"

Fargo laughed and jumped down from the wagon seat. He went to check on the other members of the wagon train. They were all right except for Otto, whose arm had been nicked by a bullet.

"It is nothing," Otto said. "A scratch. Pour a little whiskey on it, a bandage, and it will be fine."

Fargo took a look and agreed. He went back to the Ovaro and sheathed the Henry. He hoped there wouldn't be any more excitement before they got to San Antonio. Except at night. He didn't mind the kind of excitement that Michelle provided, not in the least.

Fargo collected his pay when they reached San Antonio five days later. He and Michelle broke away from the wagon train at the edge of the city and drove right to the brand-new Menger Hotel next to the old Mission San Antonio de Valero, better known as the Alamo.

"I'm sure it's a wonderful hotel," Michelle said, "but I would rather stay with you, Skye, even if it meant sleeping in the wagon."

Fargo didn't recall having gotten much sleep, but he said, "I don't think your father would like that idea."

"Bah," Michelle said, shaking her head. Her black curls bounced under her bonnet. "My father does not like any idea that I might have about men."

Fargo grinned and rubbed his hand over his short beard.

"I like your ideas just fine, myself," he said.

"But of course." Michelle gave him a brilliant smile. "How could you not?"

Fargo helped her down from the wagon, and they went into the lobby. Fargo had sent word ahead by a man on horseback they'd met along the way, and Louis Charboneau was waiting there for them, clutching his hat in front of him. He was a corpulent man with a bald head and bulging eyes, and it was clear to Fargo that Michelle must have gotten her trim figure and pretty face from her mother.

Charboneau looked like the prosperous businessman he was, quite a contrast to Fargo, who was dressed in his customary fringed buckskins and wide-brimmed brown hat, a big Colt in the holster belted at his waist, and an Arkansas Toothpick riding in its scabbard low on his leg. Yet somehow Fargo looked just as much at ease and at home as Charboneau did.

Charboneau gave a slight bow in Fargo's direction and allowed his daughter to plant a discreet kiss on the cheek. Michelle would have lingered, but her father sent her back outside.

"I have hired several men to unload your luggage," he said. "You may direct them to be sure there's no breakage. Have them take your things to your room, which is number ten. When our new house is completed, we will live there, but that will not be for another week, or so I am told."

Michelle gave Fargo a lingering look that Charboneau didn't seem to approve of before she went back outside. Fargo pretended not to notice either her look or Charboneau's reaction.

"Come, Mr. Fargo," Charboneau said after a moment. "We can have a drink, and you can tell me about your journey."

"I'll settle for my pay," Fargo said. "I have to make a call on Marshal Benson before I leave town, and I'd like to see him this afternoon."

"Very well," Charboneau said, and they went to a quiet part of the lobby where Fargo collected the money owed him.

"My daughter gave you no . . . trouble?" Charboneau said when he handed over the pay.

"Not a bit," Fargo told him. "She was very well behaved."

He didn't smile when he said it, and Charboneau seemed satisfied.

"And there were no bandits? I have heard that the trail can be dangerous."

"There were bandits, but they didn't do any damage to us. We were ready for them."

Charboneau's face darkened. "Michelle was not hurt?"

"Not a bit. She was in the wagon bed and didn't even see anything."

"That's fine, then." Charboneau relaxed and extended a damp, pudgy hand. Fargo shook it. "I wish you well, Mr. Fargo, and I appreciate the good care you took of my Michelle."

"It was my pleasure," Fargo said, and meant it.

He left the hotel and unhitched the Ovaro from the wagon. He mounted up and touched the brim of his hat when he passed Michelle, who gave him another brilliant smile as she told the men to be careful with her valises and trunks.

Fargo rode past the Alamo, where the Texicans had held off Santa Anna for thirteen days back in the war with Mexico. Now the United States Army rented the building from the Catholic Church for a hundred and fifty dollars a month. Fargo spared a thought for the brave men who had died there twenty-odd years ago, though now it didn't look much like the place where a mighty battle had been fought and lost. Or won, depending on which side you favored.

Fargo made his way through the busy city. The streets were lined with wagons pulled by mules and oxen, and the stench of their droppings filled the air. So did the smoke from blacksmith shops and the smells of leather from saddleries, the freshly sawed wood from the wagon makers, the hay and grain in the livery stables, the spicy food cooking in the open air.

Stopping at one of the livery stables, Fargo made arrangements for the Ovaro with the proprietor, a man named Fowler, and went back outside. People jostled him as he walked along the busy street. The whole place was much too crowded to suit him. He preferred the plains, mountains, prairies, deserts, and forests to the throngs of humanity in the cities. The noise from the creaking wagons, the braying mules, the hammering blacksmiths, and the talkative multitudes assaulted his ears, and he thought about the silence of a mountain night and the quiet of a desert dawn.

Then he heard the gunshots.